Cut to the Twisp

The Lost Parts of *Youth in Revolt* and Other Stories

AIVIA
PRESS

Also by C.D. Payne

Youth in Revolt: The Journals of Nick Twisp

Civic Beauties

Revolting Youth: The Further Journals of Nick Twisp

Frisco Pigeon Mambo

Queen of America (play)

Cut to the Twisp

C.D. Payne

with an appreciation by
Robert Wilonsky

AIVIA Press
www.nicktwisp.com

Sebastopol, California

Manufactured in the United States of America.

FIRST EDITION

10 9 8 7 6 5 4 3 2

"Too Young Too Late" and "Are You Camping?" originally appeared in the *Bohemian* newspaper.

Cover illustration by Joanne Applegate.

*To the people of Doubleday
who did so much to help
Nick find an audience.*

Special thanks to my agents Winifred Golden
of Castiglia Literary Agency, Del Mar,
and Jon Klane of Jon Klane Agency, Beverly Hills.

Twisp of the Tale

When C.D. Payne stopped writing ad copy, he created a revolutionary teenage hero.

By Robert Wilonsky

Contained within a care package sent by C.D. Payne is a self-penned press release introducing the author as "the Rodney Dangerfield of comic novelists," complete with a picture of the bug-eyed comedian and his shopworn catchphrase "I can't get no respect." As it turns out, this is the letter Payne sends out with all copies of his novels and plays, which he must mail himself, as he can find no publisher interested in peddling his fiction—this, despite the fact that Payne is father of one of the most beloved and iconic figures of modern literature, at least among some 25,000 readers who have adopted a precocious, if not outright dangerous, 14-year-old boy named Nick Twisp as their sex-addicted, Sinatra-obsessed god. If one needs proof of just how iconic Nick has become, consider that *Youth in Revolt*, the epic first-person novel "by" and about a boy from Oakland, California, has become a best-seller in the Czech Republic and just this month became a 10-part radio production in Germany. Then, a hero is rarely appreciated in his homeland—be his name Nick Twisp or C.D. Payne.

Payne's press release, which has landed with a thud on the cluttered desks of book reviewers around the country, offers six reasons why he should be paid attention: His first novel, a "500-page whopper" titled *Youth in Revolt*, sold more than 25,000 copies in two Doubleday editions published in the United States.

The same novel, presented in the form of Nick Twisp's diaries, has been published in five other countries; it has been turned into TV pilots for Fox and MTV, staged as a play, and broadcast on German radio; it has spawned countless Web sites and racked up more than a hundred passionately positive reviews on Amazon.com. Payne also points out that one of two new novels—*Frisco Pigeon Mambo*, about booze-swilling, chain-smoking pigeons wreaking havoc in San Francisco—is being turned into an animated feature film by the Farrelly Brothers for 20th Century Fox.

"Yeah, I write about teenagers and pigeons," Payne writes in the release for *Frisco Pigeon Mambo* and *Revolting Youth*, the sequel to *Youth in Revolt*. "No wonder I can't get respect. Anyway, here are the two latest C.D. Payne novels for you to snub."

One can far more easily detect bitterness on the printed page than over the phone: Payne's is a soft voice that barely hints at despair or disappointment, the latter of which piles around him in the form of letters from magazines and agents and publishers that have rejected his work for nearly two decades. The 51-year-old Payne—a man who has held more than two dozen jobs, from advertising copywriter to graphic artist to house remodeler to trailer-park handyman—always thought of himself as a writer even while peddling cordless phones in a catalog for gadgets and gewgaws. The publishing world has always done its best to dissuade Payne of that notion.

Seven years ago, Payne self-published 3,000 hardback editions of *Youth in Revolt*, which now sell for upward of $100 on the collector's market. It presented the journal entries of a boy who, on the verge of his 14th birthday, had become "morbidly aware of [his] penis." He despised his divorced parents (his mother dated doltish truck drivers and fascistic cops; his dad lived with a 19-year-old bimbette) and had fallen deeply in love-lust with a striking, pseudo-intellectual girl named Sheeni Saunders during a trip to a trailer park. As the novel progressed, Nick wreaked more and more havoc—burning down restaurants in Berkeley, for starters—and adopted myriad personae, including that of a would-be gangster named François Dillinger and a black-wigged woman named Carlotta Ulansky, but suffered few consequences. Indeed, the worse his actions became, the closer he got to Sheeni and satisfaction. Nick's were cathartic, comic adventures, the scribblings of a boy determined to land the girl and leave his mark—even if it were nothing but a bombed-out crater.

By the time Payne managed to sell 50 books in small bookshops around his home in California's Bay Area, he had received some five letters from readers who felt compelled to tell the author how much they identified with Nick; if nothing else, the kid did and said that which they could only imagine. It was then that Payne realized his novel, which had been spurned by legit publishers, and his teenage alter-ego, a sort of cross between Bart Simpson and François Truffaut's Antoine Doinel and Philip Roth's Alexander Portnoy, were taking hold. In 1995, Doubleday published a hardback copy of the novel and sent the author on a small promotional book tour; the paperback version is in its sixth edition.

"I think the fun thing about Nick is, he doesn't get discouraged by the knocks that life hands him," Payne says. "He's almost like a cartoon character in that respect, and there's very little filtering between his impulses and his actions. He's just always out there, ready to do just about anything, and that's kind of fun to hang around with a character like that. That may be why book editors don't understand Nick. He doesn't fit in the standard mold. Fact is, he could be a real guy, and the thing that sort of amazed me about the reaction of readers is that they do take Nick so seriously and they identify with Nick. The fact that it's skirting the edge of reality doesn't really seem to bother them. They accept Nick as a real person. That came as a real surprise to me.

"I was just exaggerating things for comic effect. I do what comic authors do, and I know that you have to have at least some basis in reality, but I thought that I was taking Nick into fairly unbelievable territory, but readers don't seem to feel that way about him. It's kind of an aging baby boomer's fantasy of contemporary teen life. I certainly didn't think that kids today would identify with him. Somebody pointed out to me they liked it because the parents are so stupid, and Nick is sort of at an age where he's pretty powerless, and yet he does escape the realm of his parents."

Appropriately, *Youth in Revolt* became the subject of much interest in Hollywood, which sought to turn the novel into a TV series or a film. In 1996, Fox-TV actually filmed a pilot—starring Christopher Masterson as Nick and Jane Kaczmarek as his mother, both of whom would end up starring in Fox's Malcolm in the Middle—but so altered the premise that it would have been unrecognizable to the book's fans. Nick no longer adored Sinatra; instead, he worshipped Captain and Tennille. Fox declined to pick up the show, despite Payne's insistence that he kind of liked it, and MTV picked up the option. But the writer who penned the MTV pilot drowned in a boating accident shortly after he turned in the script, and the project has since withered at the music network.

Then, when Payne gave Doubleday the sequel to *Youth in Revolt*, *Revolting Youth*, the publisher declined. Other publishers had no interest in selling a sequel to a book they hadn't originally been involved in, so he was forced, once more, to self-publish. Indeed, all of Payne's subsequent works—including *Frisco Pigeon Mambo* and the play *Queen of America*, which offers an alternate reality based upon George Washington's decision to become king instead of president—have been issued through Payne's own Aivia Press, based out of Sebastopol, California. Payne (who also maintains his own Web site, www.nicktwisp.com) shrugs off the series of disasters and disappointments: Just my luck.

But he knows why he is doomed to enjoy the accolades of the cult: He is a vestige, a comic novelist long after the form has withered on the shelf; as a result, he likes to say he was born 50 years too late, referring to himself as "a throwback." He spent the first 15 years of his writing career penning short pieces, which he would send off to *The New Yorker*—"and talk about being out of date," Payne says, chuckling softly. He racked up numerous rejections from the magazine, but did wind up selling it a cartoon that was illustrated by Charles Addams; it was a small reward for seven years' worth of effort. He also landed two stories with *Esquire*, which published only one before notifying him that the magazine was changing formats and would no longer run humor tales. He turned to writing novels only as a last resort; it was either that or go back to school "to study accounting or something."

Nick was hatched in one of those early short pieces: Payne penned a "letter" from Nick to his parents, in which he detailed his first 13 years. But by 1989, Payne decided to write about Nick in a novel—which over a three-year period became three novels, bound in a single volume and titled *Youth in Revolt*. Payne had no intention of writing a second novel about Nick, and he says that if there is a third, it would be "a miracle." Indeed, he wrote *Revolting Youth* for two reasons: He wanted to ride alongside Nick and see where the boy would take him, and he wanted to give something to the fans and fetishists who have made an obscure literary creation their revolutionary sweetheart.

"That is probably the thing that's kept me going," Payne says of his rabid, ravenous fans. "Literally every 20 minutes, I would decide to hang up the typewriter—in this case, the computer—and get on with my life and do something else. I still think that probably several times a week, just because I've gotten so many knocks along the way. That's the thing that sustains me. I've read a lot of books in my life, and I think I've only written one fan letter to one author, so when I started receiving them, I thought, 'Gee, this is kinda strange to hear from all these people when I've sold only a handful of books.' It's Nick's readership that has kept me going. Definitely. But really, I just write Nick for myself, and so far I haven't been writing to please book editors—and God forbid I should ever do that—and I figure the readers are going to have to take it or leave it. I don't know quite where I got this attitude from. Maybe it's from being knocked around so much."

Kind of like Nick Twisp.

Reprinted from the *Dallas Observer*. ©2001 New Times. All rights reserved. Used with permission.

The Lost Parts of *Youth in Revolt*

These passages were cut from the 1995 and later U.S. editions on the pages indicated:

[Page 19, after "living hell."] Of course, he searches her room every time she leaves the house, but nothing has turned up so far. She left an armed mouse trap in her panties drawer, but he saw it just in time. He moved it two drawers down, and right as he was leaving he heard a snap, followed by a piercing scream.

8:30 p.m. Lefty just called, sounding worried. I could barely hear him over Barry in the background warbling "Bali Hai" at concert volume. Martha has two bruised fingers and war has been declared.

[Page 35, after "siren wailing."] I wondered if I would be sent to the California Youth Authority for this first offense. There to be brutally gang-raped and to contract AIDS. I would be dead before I was 20—never to have had a sexual experience with a woman under age 79. With nothing to lose now, I ordered a cream-filled chocolate old-fashioned. Zits were the least of my worries.

[Page 35, after "countered the geezer."] They agreed on $910, with the seller writing out a false bill of sale for $200 to save on sales tax at the DMV. Mom, as a salaried employee of the Department of Motor Vehicles, looked a bit uncomfortable about this, but did not object.

[Page 49, after "blue neon fish."] Biff himself greeted us in the fishing net-draped lobby. I knew it was Biff because all over the walls were framed photographs of him shaking hands with Famous Celebrities. I recognized Regis Philbin, Barbie Benton, Al Gore, and—believe it or not—Frank Sinatra, Jr. After brazenly eyeing my date, Biff led us to our table—a choice one beside the windows. Biff held Sheeni's seat out for her and casually laid a liver-spotted paw on her bare shoulder as he was handing her a menu. In retaliation, as I was taking my seat I ground my heel into his toes. After that, I thought, Biff looked at me with new respect.

[Page 50, after "ordered steaks."] Jerry asked for his medium, so I asked for medium rare, so he asked for medium rare, so I switched to rare, so he decided on rare too. Since I didn't want to eat raw cow the competition stopped there. Surprisingly, both of our steaks arrived grilled a perfect medium rare. (Perhaps it was something Mom whispered to the waitress.) We also had French bread with butter, corn muffins with butter, buttered asparagus, and baked potatoes with butter and sour cream. Butter also appeared to be melting on the sizzling steaks when they arrived. Alas, there was no butter in the salad—only sour cream and blue cheese.

[Page 57, after "alone and numb."] The trip back was ineffably sad. We picked up the trailer without a hitch, or should I say, without a mishap. In the harsh light of day it looked much shabbier than it had in the dimness of the shed—especially shackled to the shiny white Lincoln. We looked like the new poor—forced by circumstance to flee California, perhaps to take up tenant farming in rural Oklahoma. As we drove off, the geezer waved and called out, "Happy trailering!" I couldn't help but wonder if that comment was made tongue in cheek. Perhaps it was just my state of mind.

[Page 59, after "Trent rates higher."] I went up to my room and sorted through my meager stack of mail. Thank God, Dad came through with an allowance check. Now I can buy dog food. Joanie sent a chatty letter and a newspaper clipping. Seems a guy in Florida slid into the handlebars when his motorcycle hit a wall at 50 mph. The reconstructive surgery failed and now he wears a dress, answers to the name of Susan, and is engaged to a former Boy Scout chum. They're planning to adopt. He says probably none of these good things would have happened if he'd been wearing a helmet. "The brain damage improved my emotional flexibility," he told UPI.

I cringed and checked my equipment to make sure it was still intact. It looked OK. I checked the erect length. Up one-quarter inch—I'm now officially average! I checked the ejaculatory system. Still works like a charm. I just hope (for Sheeni's sake), my hydraulic pressure doesn't blast a hole through *Consumer's* check-rated condom.

[Page 62, after "Lacey's fabulous bod."] She is a kick to watch in a restaurant. All the waiters fawn over her, so she adopts an attitude somewhere between the Empress of China and the Queen of Sheeba. She demanded a better table, complained her menu was "soiled," sent back her bottled water ("it's not Evian, I can tell"), sent back her water again ("didn't I tell you? No ice"), sent back her salad ("too lemony"), sent back her salmon ("bring me one without bones"), and demanded a dessert that wasn't on the menu ("sliced fresh fruit with honey and yogurt").

The waiters only got snotty once—when Dad tried to send back the chardonnay. They tasted it, pronounced the wine "absolutely superb," and refused to bring a new bottle. So Dad had to drink the "vile vinegar" while seething inwardly. Then there was another ugly scene when the head waiter and the manager refused to take the wine off the tab. (Their brilliant argument: the wine couldn't have been too undrinkable, since Dad and Lacey polished off the entire bottle.) To get back at them, as we were leaving Dad casually dropped the wine bucket over the balcony. But they saw him do it, and made him pay for that too. What a delightfully relaxing meal!

Then Dad didn't feel like driving "all the way back to Oakland," so he dropped me off at a BART station. I didn't get home until after 10 p.m. Mom had already gone to bed.

[Page 77, after "she sat down."] Later, at the home of the grieving family a light buffet was served. I was shocked to see the refreshments included asparagus, a vegetable for which Lefty reserved his fiercest loathing, and which his sister invariably served when she made dinner. Even on this day of mourning, I noticed, Martha could not resist the vile green spears. She looked up and paused in mid-chew.

"Hello, Nick," she said glumly.

"Hi, Martha," I said. "How's the asparagus?"

"Mmmm, very good," she replied, resuming her dispirited mastication.

"So," I said, after a pause. "Heard any new Barry Coma records lately?"

Martha turned white. "What, what did you say?" she stammered.

"Oddest thing," I said. "I had a dream about Lefty last night. He appeared—dripping wet and ghostly pale—and asked me to ask you that."

Crash! Martha's plate shattered against the tile floor. She turned and bolted from the room.

[Page 80, after "prayer meeting."] "Then this evening Rev. Knuddlesdopper's faction had a barbecue in his honor on the lawn by the bath house. Lefty ate four hamburgers, five ears of corn, half a German chocolate cake, and, in between bites, talked about his native land."

"My God, what did he say?" I asked. "I doubt if Lefty even knows what planet Burma is on."

"He said quite a lot," Sheeni replied. "Let's see. He said the national sport was volleyball, although video games were big too. He said chili dogs were the national dish. He said that most of the people were poor and could only afford to drive Toyotas and Plymouths. Oh, and he said if sisters became obnoxious, boys in the family had the legal right to send them away to convents—for life."

[Page 95, after "school tuition."] Mom unwrapped one package in the living room—a large, framed color photograph of her deceased paramour, which she hung above the fireplace. From this hallowed vantage point, Jerry can gaze down for eternity upon his penultimate automobile and the rebellious youth who loathed him.

[Page 107, after "on that track!"] And so, without any conditioning, without any preliminary stretching, 30 African-American youths and I did eight laps of the track. Then six more. I thought I was going to faint. Back in the locker room, I was among the last to hold onto my breakfast. But as the world heaved around me, my three chocolate cream donuts lost their grip and joined the fragrant buffet on the floor. Still, sick as we were, the whip-cracking overseer made us all take showers. Was my pale winkie the most abbreviated in the room? Does the Pope serve refreshments on Sundays?

[Page 109, after "attention to me."] I spent most of the morning getting caught up on all the computer magazines. Then I started to feel somewhat guilty, so I took down a book on biology and read it awhile. Very boring stuff. Next I had a nice lunch at McDanold's. Then I went back and mined the fiction section for dirty passages. All and all, I think I improved my mind considerably more than I would have at school. And it was ever so much more pleasant. Perhaps I am destined to be one of those great self-educated renaissance men.

[Page 112, after "stimulating day at the library.] With the nice weather we've been having, most of the homeless were outdoors working on their tans. So the library was pleasantly uncrowded with only occasional pockets of bad b.o. And some of the most malodorous offenders were library personnel themselves. What a collection of dispirited, ill-garbed misfits. They really have no excuse either, since the library subscribes to both *Vogue* and *GQ*. I think a monthly perusal of those magazines should be compulsory for all employees (and perhaps the homeless as well).

[Page 112, after "unexpanded) mind."] Seeking more variety in my diet, I went to Burger Prince for lunch. I must confess I felt a little nervous gazing at the minimum-wage burger jockeys as I munched my fries. How many of them were once-budding intellectuals who dropped out of stultifying public schools? I may consider myself a self-educated renaissance man, but what if the world views me only as an ninth-grade dropout? Will Sheeni be embarrassed to introduce me to her highbrow Parisian friends? Will Knopf return my manuscripts unread? Will I be flipping spatulas instead of signing autographs? The conclusion is inescapable: at some point soon I shall have to rejoin the educational establishment.

[Page 113, after "degenerate dweeb."] "I found her diary again," noted Lefty. "It was taped inside the furnace duct."

"Anything spicy?"

"Jalapeño City, as usual. Guess who she's got the hots for now?" he asked.

"Me?"

"Dream on. You're off about 30 years. It's Dr. Browerly."

"Your shrink?" I exclaimed.

"Yep. And boy does she want him bad—wrinkles, bald head, and all."

"How do you know that?" I asked.

"She says when she leaves his office her panties are drenched with desire. That was the word she used, 'drenched.' In fact, she's thinking of mailing him a pair."

"Jesus, Lefty, your sister's crazy."

"You can say that again," agreed Lefty. "It's a good thing she's going to a psychologist."

[Page 114, after "hanging around my mother."] He is making some progress though (romantically speaking). Mom has removed Jerry's memorial portrait from its place of honor over the fireplace and hung it in the back hallway next to the laundry room. How quickly are the deceased prised from the hearts of the living. I am resolved to avoid this through a clever strategy—I shall simply outlive all my loved ones.

[Page 115, after "evolve into a man-eater."] The chilly weather has brought throngs of literature-mad homeless back into the library. I wonder if anyone would object if I pursued my self-education there with a clothespin on my nose? After lunch, to escape the stench, I went on a one-man field trip to the thrift shops in Oakland's Chinatown. I found a nice pair of real pearl earrings for Sheeni for 35 cents, a switchblade comb for ten cents, a slightly scratched F.S. album for a buck, and a pair of genuine surgical steel gynecological forceps (at least I think that's what it is) for five dollars. Since I didn't have five dollars, I was obliged to make this last purchase via Lefty's discount strategy.

Boy, is larceny nerve wracking. No wonder people go into white-collar crime instead. The forceps, though, were definitely worth the risk. They are wonderfully erotic to fondle and a great confidence booster. There's nothing like having the proper professional instruments on hand in case someone cute invites you to play doctor.

[Page 116, after "on his bedroom door."] Under the bedclothes, gynecological forceps were clamped to my erect member.

"I have a message for you from Lefty," she growled.

"What is it?" I asked, nonchalantly leaning forward and raising my knees. The cold steel bit into my groin.

[Page 116, after "September 15."] The day dawned warm, sunny, and beautiful. A great day for tossing a baseball around in the park. Thank God I'm devoutly unathletic. Otherwise, I'm sure I'd feel the pain of 30 dreary days in the hole even more acutely.

[Page 119, after "Then what did you do?"] "Well, you know she wants to be an anesthesiologist when she grows up. So we walked down to Herrick Hospital and hung out in the emergency room for a while."

"How was that?"

"Not bad. There was a neat stabbing victim they brought in with the sirens going. Blood all over the place. He lived though."

[Page 127, after "beginning to thaw."] Sitting beside her, I could admire her new pearl earrings. When I presented them to her, Sheeni exclaimed, "Oh, Nick, genuine clip-on faux pearl earrings. How exquisitely retro!" I knew she'd like them.

[Page 130, after "suspend our consultations."] "That would be tragic," I agreed. "Maybe you could send him something else in the mail in case Mom's check doesn't come through."

"What do you mean?" demanded Martha.

"Nothing," I said. "Can I speak to Lefty?"

"The dweeb went up to Tilden Park," she replied. "And what did you mean by that?"

"Forget it, Martha. See you around."

The receiver was still squawking when I hung it up. Uh-oh, I thought, loose lips sink ships.

[Page 132, after "disquieting phone call from Lefty."] I could barely hear him over Barry in the background crooning "Til the

End of Time." Martha is back on the warpath. And Millie Filbert has terminated their relationship. Unfairly, my friend blames me for both of these developments.

[Page 132, after "my girlfriend's body!"] And what are you going to do about Martha?"

"That's easy," I replied. "Tell Martha if she doesn't can the music you'll be compelled to reveal the contents of her diary to Dr. Browerly. That should get her off your back. And stop snooping in your sister's damn diary. You should respect other people's privacy."

"Look who's talking!" exclaimed Lefty.

He had a point there. Even François grudgingly conceded that.

[Page 134, after "throbbing in my shoulder."] So after Lefty stopped by for the letter, I crawled into bed and spent many miserable hours in deepest ennui-land. Around 3:30 I was startled out of my delirium by a light tapping on my door.

"Yes?" I croaked.

The door opened slightly. "Can I come in?" asked a hesitant female voice.

"Why not?" I replied. "Everyone else does."

The door swung open and Millie Filbert walked in. Fresh from the rigors of private school, she was wearing a neat forest green skirt and simple white blouse. A stack of books was cradled in her arms against her left breast. Oh, to be a ninth-grade math textbook, I thought.

"Hi, Millie," I exclaimed, startled.

"Hi, Nick," she said. "The door was open downstairs so I let myself in. I hope I'm not disturbing you."

"Not at all. Come in."

Millie smiled shyly and walked over. "I hope you're feeling better."

"A little," I replied weakly. "Nice to see you. Have a seat."

Millie put down her books and sat on the edge of the bed. (Brazenly ignoring the nearby chair!) "That was a very nice note you wrote me, Nick," she said. "You have an excellent vocabulary."

"Thank you, Millie," I replied. "I've always admired your . . . vocabulary as well." I liked the way her lacy bra showed through the sheer fabric of the blouse.

"I'm sorry I kicked you yesterday, Nick."

"Quite all right. I deserved it. I had no business spying on you and Lefty."

"Did you see very much?"

"No," I lied, "my view was blocked by some foliage."

"Oh," said Millie, sounding disappointed. She reached out a pale white hand and touched the bandage on my forehead. "Does it hurt much, Nick?"

"Nothing I can't stand," I replied bravely.

Millie smiled. "I like a man in bandages."

"Yes. Lefty has remarked you want to be an anesthesiologist someday."

"I ask you," said Millie earnestly, "what profession relieves more pain?"

"I can't think of any," I admitted.

Millie gazed around the room, no doubt admiring my mottled green and khaki wall treatment. "Is this your girlfriend?" she asked, pointing to the photo of Sheeni pinned to the wall above my bed.

"Uh, well, she's not really my girlfriend," I was amazed to hear François reply. "I hardly know her really."

"Then why do you have her picture on your wall?"

"Oh, I like the stylistic composition of the visual elements in that photograph."

"So you don't have a girlfriend, Nick?" asked Millie.

François put a warm hand on Millie's exquisite knee. "No, but I'd like one," he said.

Millie leaned toward me and whispered, "You, uh. You don't have a baseball card collection do you, Nick?"

"Not at all," I replied. "Sports bore me."

"Well, outdoor sports," added François.

Millie smiled and leaned even closer, applying a soothing breast to my injured shoulder. "Is there anything I can do for you, Nick?"

"How about unbuttoning your blouse," replied François.

"Certainly," said Millie. She unbuttoned her blouse, removed it, and folded it neatly on a corner of the bed. Her milky white breasts swelled above the constricting lace.

"Does that bra unsnap from the front?" asked François.

"Yes," replied Millie, demonstrating how it worked. "I find this design much more convenient." She folded the brassiere and placed it on top of the blouse. I marveled at her neatness.

"If you take off your skirt, we could play doctor," suggested François.

"That's a great idea," agreed Millie. "But you have to remove your pajamas too."

"It's a deal!" Hindered by my stiff shoulder, I was much slower than Millie in shedding my clothes. She stepped out of her skirt and panties, then helped me remove my pajama bottoms. Moving her hand slowly up my thigh, she gently grasped my swollen rod and examined it with professional interest.

"This growth looks serious," said Millie. "Does it hurt?"

"It aches for you," replied François, thrilled by her touch. "Now let me examine you."

"Certainly, doctor." Releasing her grip, Millie lay back on the rumpled bed and shyly opened her legs. Under the triangle of dense black hair, a sheen of moisture glistened on her delicate. . .

The door flew open and Mom walked in. "What do you think you're doing?" she exclaimed.

"Typing on my computer," I replied.

"Get back in bed! You're supposed to be resting."

So I got back into bed. And I never even got to the part where I took out the gleaming forceps. Yes, diary, I confess. This account of Millie's visit was complete fiction. Well, I told you it was a boring day.

[Page 134, after "a fat policeman."] I just had another unpleasant shock. Someone knocked on my door, I said "enter," and beaming Rhonda Atari waddled in. Talk about kicking a guy when he's down. It's bad enough coping with her cloying ministrations in public, let alone having to confront her in one's very own private chambers. I'm afraid François was not very polite.

"Hi, Nick!" she bubbled. "How are you feeling?"

"The doctors give me one more week at the most," replied François weakly. "What do you want?"

Rhonda beamed. "Oh, Nick, you're so funny. Your mother told me you don't have a brain tumor at all. And I was so worried. You have a strained shoulder and poison oak. No one dies from that."

"What do you want, Rhonda?" repeated François.

"Oh, I brought you all your homework," she said, dumping a frighteningly large stack of books and papers on my desk. "I'm afraid you're getting a little behind."

"You'll never have that problem," commented François. "Yours is immense."

"Gee, what's wrong with your walls?" asked Rhonda, ignoring the gibe and scrutinizing my private sanctuary uninvitedly.

"I painted them during one of my psychotic states," explained François. "I prefer a hallucinogenic environment."

"Oh, Nick, you're so weird," said Rhonda, clearly implying she found weirdness extremely endearing. "Who's this person in the photo?"

"That is the one great and magnificent love of my life," replied François. "Isn't she beautiful?"

Rhonda's crest had clearly fallen. "She's OK. She looks kind of dumb though."

"Oh, quite the contrary. She is by far the most intelligent person I have ever met."

"Well, she doesn't look very truthful," said Rhonda, obviously clutching at straws. "Her eyes are kind of shifty like."

"Her eyes are shimmering azure pools of deep sincerity," I countered. "She is altogether wonderful. In fact, we're engaged to be married."

"You are no such thing," insisted Rhonda. "You're too young to be engaged."

"That is your opinion, of course," said François. "Not that the matter is of any concern to you."

"I don't care who you go and marry," she announced. "I'm going to study hard, go to college, and get a good paying job before I get married. By then, you'll probably be divorced and paying alimony!"

"I think not," said François. "Sheeni and I are destined to cleave for all time."

"Well, Nick, I hope your cleaving doesn't interfere with doing your homework. You've got lots. And personally, I think IBM computers are boring!"

With that, Rhonda activated her immense bodily mass and flounced out.

I must insist to Mom that she screen my visitors. I'm not a well person.

[Page 144, after "learning to drive."] 7:30 p.m. Mom looks distracted. She made Swiss steak and fried potatoes tonight for dinner—even though it is a truth universally acknowledged that Swiss steak is to be served with *mashed* potatoes. Of course, I prefer fried potatoes, which makes her choice even stranger. No boyfriends were invited. Mom laments her food bills have gone "out of sight." When I filled her in on the latest developments in the "Lance Wescott, Ace Detective" saga, her only comment was, "Gee, it's a good thing Joanie didn't marry Phil Polsetta, even though married life can be wonderful."

Mom must have an elastically forgetful memory to say that with a straight face. Is it possible she is contemplating cinching the love bridle on Husband Number Two? If so, who will be the lucky guy? And will he treat his new stepson with deference, respect, and courtesy? These questions haunt me.

[Page 163, after "that is the question?"] On the one hand, it is incontrovertibly true that two days ago I started a fire in Berkeley that caused $5 million in damages. At least my alter ego François started it. (I have been forced by circumstances to split my personality in half: 14-year-old Nick Twisp is in charge of flossing daily, improving our minds, dressing conservatively, and acting respectfully toadyish around adults. Reckless, darkly handsome François Dillinger takes care of swearing, holding authority in contempt, flaunting conventional sexual mores, and projecting a sense of menacing danger.)

On the other hand, my loathsome father, under whose despotic rule I have come to live while hiding out from the arson investigators, has not stated explicitly that I *am* grounded. Of course, I dare not ask him. As a test, after lunch I announced I was taking my dog Albert (named by my intellectual girlfriend, Sheeni Saunders, after the late existentialist Albert Camus) for a walk into town. Dad did not object. He did not comment at all, but continued to gaze fixedly at the sheerly draped bosom of Lacey, his alluring 19-year-old live-in bimbette. (I spend a lot of time gazing at her too; she's an incredible knockout.)

So, until told otherwise, I am proceeding under the assumption that I am free to do as I please. What a change from the endless weeks of solitary confinement suffered under my tyrannical mother in Oakland and her vile cop boyfriend Lance Wescott. Freedom is wonderful—even if all you're free to do is walk four hot, dusty miles into Ukiah, California: gateway to Mendocino County's clear-cut redwood groves.

This was my first look at my new home town, hallowed birthplace of The Woman I Love. Yes, I still love Sheeni. Even though she lured me here with promises of sweet sexual delights, and then promptly transferred (along with her allegedly former boyfriend Trent) to a Frog-speaking boarding school hundreds of miles away in Santa Cruz.

[Page 167, after "secondhand parental tars."] 10:10 p.m. Lacey, dressed provocatively for bed (I don't see how Dad gets any sleep at all), just knocked on my door to tell me I had a call. I prayed it was Sheeni.

"I hate your slimy guts," said a voice. It was my old Oakland pal Lefty, whose trek beyond virginity I have been assisting. Despite his notoriety as the Bay Area's best-known teen Peyronie's disease victim, Lefty has on two recent occasions nearly united his eccentrically curvilinear member with the more conventionally curvaceous Millie Filbert. Success, he believes, would render unnecessary the penile corrective surgery his parents are clamoring for.

"What's the problem now?" I asked.

"Millie dumped me for Clive Bosendorf!" he exclaimed.

"Clive Bosendorf!" I replied, incredulous. "That midget's only three feet tall."

"You're telling me," complained Lefty. "He comes right up to her chest."

That may be far enough, I thought. I said, "She's only playing with you, Lefty. She's still a little angry about your being arrested in bed together. She'll get over it. She can't be serious about a shrimp like Clive."

"Well, they were holding hands at lunch today! I nearly threw up."

"Did you threaten Clive?" I asked.

"Of course," said Lefty in despair. "But he said if I pounded him, he'd blab to Millie."

"He would too, the little worm. Well, Lefty, what can I do about it? I'm 150 miles away."

"You could write to Millie. Tell her it was your fault the cops interrupted us."

"OK, I guess I could do that," I replied, not pointing out that the fault undoubtedly lay elsewhere. How was I to know Mom's perfidious cop boyfriend was going to raid the house for burglars just as Lefty was swinging for home plate up in my room?

"But, Lefty," I cautioned, "don't expect much from the letter. The way to get Millie back is to act indifferent. Women hate that."

"But I'm not indifferent," he complained, "I'm deeply in love."

"Yes, and Millie can sense it. That's why she's torturing you. What you've got to do is give her back some of her own medicine. I suggest you put the moves on some other chick."

"Like who?" he demanded.

"Anyone will do. Just make sure she's smart, popular, good-looking, and stacked. Otherwise, Millie might not get sufficiently jealous."

"Yeah," said Lefty, brightening, "and if she's that good, I might not want Millie back at all!"

"Oh, uh, sure," I said, somewhat shocked.

It's guys like Lefty who give teen romance its unfortunate reputation for shoddy insincerity.

[Page 167, after "panic under control."] Kindhearted Lacey gave me a lift to school this morning. Dad could, but he thinks the one-hour walk each way is just what I need. Wait, though, until he has to buy me a new pair of shoes. We're so far out in the boonies, I may go through a pair a week at this rate.

Lacey drives (recklessly) the ubiquitous single career woman's budget Toyota. Not since Studebaker went belly up have cars been this boring. At least the driver is the deluxe, grand tourisimo sports model.

On the way, I asked Lacey if she minded Dad's non-stop criticisms, sarcastic comments, and put-downs.

"It gets on my nerves a lot," she admitted. "I wish George could relax for two seconds just once. You'd think all that booze would calm him down a little. Nope. He's like one big raw, exposed nerve ending 24 hours a day."

I had to ask. "Why do you put up with it?" It seemed to me Lacey could have her choice of any man on the planet.

"Oh, I don't know," she replied. "He's kinda cute. And he's real smart."

I guess when so many of your genes are devoted to alluring sexuality there aren't many left over to handle critical discernment.

[Page 168, after "run of one-dish meals."] After cleaning up the kitchen (Lacey helped), I penned this missive to Millie Filbert:

Dear Millie,

Greetings from the Redwood Empire! Life up here on Dad's ranch is certainly a big change from the city. I just finished grooming Fire Walker, my Arabian stallion, and thought I'd catch up on some of my correspondence. I was shocked and appalled to hear of your unfortunate encounter with the Oakland police. Lefty tells me you acted with magnificent poise. He continues to express admiration for your unwavering courage through the grim trials of that traumatic evening. We are all taking strength from your sterling example.

Just for the record I'd like to confirm what I'm sure you must have concluded, that is, that both Lefty and I were entirely ignorant of the police surveillance of my home and thus cannot be held accountable in any way for the ensuing misunderstanding. I know I may rely on your sense of fair play to preclude any other possible interpretation of those events.

Lefty informs me happily that you have befriended little Clive Bosendorf. He is charmed by your goodwill toward the height-challenged and sees this as yet another confirmation of your innate beneficence. His admiration for you continues to bloom, even as circumstances have kept you apart. He prays earnestly this separation may be short-lived.

I have added French to my studies this year and find it a marvelously expressive language. Of course, I do greatly miss not sharing Miss Satron's English Literature class with you and Lefty. My regards to you all. I remain as ever . . .

your pal,

Nick Twisp

That's it for this night. Except for some grooming attention to a T.E. that's begun to kick angrily in its stalls. Time to take Fire Walker out for a canter. This magnificent stallion I ride bareback—hanging on with one hand.

[Page 168, after "virginity last year."] Despite the heat, I did retain sufficient mental agility to achieve a near perfect 98 on a physics test—the top score in the class. I could feel the dagger-like glances of my fellow students as Mr. Tratinni (a genuinely nice man) singled me out for praise. No doubt about it, I have established myself as an academic force to be reckoned with. Even the Zit Queen looked at me with new respect.

[Page 171, after "I doubt it."] 9:30 p.m. Dad just barged into my room without knocking and yelled at me to turn off "that repulsive music."

"But, Dad, it's Frank Sinatra," I said. Frank was at that moment crooning through the great Jerome Kern classic "The Song Is You."

"It sucks," said Dad. "If you want to play that garbage, listen through your headphones."

Reluctantly, I turned down the volume. Why are parents such fascistic stick-in-the-muds when it comes to their children's taste in music?

[Page 173, after "meet Mr. Preston himself."] What an enchanting man! Tall and distinguished, he combines the elegant looks of a mature Cary Grant with the friendliness of Dale Carnegie, the manners of a renaissance courtier, the compassion of Albert Schweitzer, and the authoritative competence of Walter Cronkite. If only he'd had a courtly and compassionate vasectomy in his youth. Or, failing that, had met my mother before Dad stumbled on the scene. Am I saying I wish Mr. Preston had been my father? Does the Pope kiss airport asphalt?

[Page 174, after "endearingly unintelligible word!"] After struggling without success to decipher it, I put the scented missive aside to open my second letter. This too was written in a charming feminine hand. It read:

Dear Nick,

Not that it's any of your business, but Clive Bosendorf happens to be a great guy. He's also grown two full inches since he started getting hormone injections this summer. By Christmas he expects to be taller than all you turkeys. So watch out!

I suppose I should thank you for showing me what a total zero Lefty is. When the Vice Squad broke in on us he acted like a spineless wimp. I was never so humiliated in all my life. I wouldn't go out with that jerk again if he was the last boy on Earth. I hear he's putting the moves on Wanda Fletcher. I could tell you some things about that b----h, but I'm not going to waste our country's finite paper resources.

I'm going to soccer camp in Hopland this weekend, so I'll call you Saturday night to come see your ranch. I love horses and would like to get a ride on Fire Walker. Don't worry, I got your phone number from a certain deformed wimp.

Regards,

Millie

Incredulous, I read that last paragraph three times. Each time the message remained the same. Millie Filbert is coming to visit me today. Why does this thought make my hands tremble? Why do I suddenly have The T.E. That Devoured Fresno?

[Page 175, after "buy a bike like that?"] Vijay evinced polite interest in our residence. "A portable manufactured house. How intriguing. I've seen them, but have never been in one before. The rooms are surprisingly spacious. But why are the walls so obviously simulated wood? Does it really fool people?"

I replied that we Americans feel more comfortable in surroundings that are safely distanced from nature. "It has to do with issues of control," I explained. "We like to feel that nature is subjugated to our will at all times."

Vijay was more enthusiastic about Lacey.

[Page 177, after "devote to Great Ideas."] 6:10 p.m. Millie just called. Right as I was finishing the dinner dishes. She has a "horrible bruise" (from getting kicked in the leg at soccer camp), but is still sufficiently ambulatory for her ranch tour if not her stallion ride. I broke the news that an unfortunate outbreak of hoof and mouth disease had put the ranch under quarantine, but offered to sneak out to meet her downtown. She was disappointed, but agreed to the plan. Lacey has volunteered to give me a lift. I changed my clothes and François pocketed a condom just in case. He also slipped in Millie's brassiere (left behind in the police raid) as a conversational icebreaker.

11:40 p.m. I'm back. What a night! I'm too overwrought to sleep so I might as well get the story down on microchip. Millie, looking tantalizingly sunburned (does flawless alabaster skin not tan?), was lounging as specified in front of Flampert's variety store. She had dressed for the occasion in jeans, a brand new I GET A KICK OUT OF HOPLAND soccer camp tee-shirt, sandals, and scarlet toenail polish. All too evidently, I was the only person packing a bra.

"Well, Nick," said Millie brightly, "what's there to do in this town?"

"Uh, not much, Millie. We could go for a walk. I could buy you an ice cream."

"That sounds nice."

So we walked slowly up and down the empty streets in the warm twilight. We looked in the thrift store and dress shop windows, studied the array of washing machines and chain saws behind the plate glass in the Sears catalog store, peered into the noisy bars, examined the property-for-sale listings in the windows of real estate offices, commiserated with a nervous-looking rabbit sharing the front window of a reptile store with an immense boa constrictor, and—as darkness fell—refreshed ourselves with two triple-dip ice cream cones served up by a hostile youth in a ridiculous paper hat. From his manner I could tell he thought in a perfect world I would be scooping up the confections and he would be squiring the knockout brunette.

As we walked, licked, and wiped (our cones and lips respectively), Millie continued to ask me probingly knowledgeable equestrian-related questions. I continued to answer haltingly (why hadn't I been at the library all this afternoon boning up on Arabian horseflesh?), while endeavoring to steer the conversation back to her misjudged boyfriend Lefty.

"I don't think Lefty is a wimp at all," I declared.

"Oh, Nickie," replied Millie, "how can you say that?"

The appellation "Nickie" had been a recent, stimulating addition to our conversation. To match the pace, I had accelerated to "Mil."

"Well, for one thing, Mil, he may just be the best damn shoplifter in the state."

"OK, so the creep's a thief too. There are lots of wimps in San Quentin."

Clearly an unsubstantiated assertion, but I let the point drop for now. Millie's sugar cone had begun to drip from the tip onto her nice new tee-shirt. As the drips were falling in a provocative area, modesty prevented me from bringing it to her attention. François had no such scruples.

"Be careful, Mil," he said. "Your cone is dripping on your left breast area."

"Fuck!" she exclaimed, handing me her soggy cone and daubing the stains with her napkin. "I just got this shirt today!"

"Don't worry," I said. "The stains should wash out. It looks like a polyester blend."

"Not that I know anything about laundering fabrics," added François, mentally kicking me.

"No, you're probably right," she said. "Oh, throw that away!"

So François dropped the remains of Millie's cone on the sidewalk. The ever-frugal Nick went on eating his as they turned down a dark residential street. Crunching into the cone, he resumed his advocacy of his friend.

"What about the time in fifth grade when Lefty saved my life?"

"Lefty saved your life?" asked Millie, surprised.

"Yes," I lied. "Why do you suppose we're such great pals?"

Our stroll had brought us to an elementary school, looming anxiously in the black night like long division.

"Oh, Nickie, let's go swing on the swings!"

Millie grabbed my hand and led me toward the deserted playground. Lefty was right—her hand was warm and not at all clammy. While I sat on a swing and discussed Lefty's heroism, Millie soared back and forth in the dark.

"And so you see," I said, "if Lefty hadn't stopped the runaway bulldozer, the tent I was sleeping in would have been crushed."

Millie slowed slightly. "How did the bulldozer get started in the first place?"

"I told you. Some of the other Cub Scouts in camp started it."

"How can a kid start a giant bulldozer?"

"I suppose the loggers must have left the key in it by mistake."

"So Lefty jumped up on a moving bulldozer? That doesn't sound much like him. Why didn't he just get you out of the tent instead?"

"Well, there were more tents in its path farther on. The dozer had to be stopped at any cost."

"Oh, I see," said Millie. "So Lefty saved other people's lives that day too?"

"Oh sure. He was a real hero. They were thinking of renaming the camp after him, but it would have jeopardized their federal funding."

"Did you have horses at the camp?"

This woman has a one track mind, I thought. "No, just pack llamas," I lied. "Boy, you can sure swing."

"I was my grammar school champion," Millie announced. "Try it."

I tried, but concluded strenuous swinging was not an activity to do with a stomach full of melted ice cream. As I slowed, Millie spotted something dangling from my back pocket.

"What's that?" she asked, stopping.

This was François' cue. "Oh, Mil, it's your brassiere," he said. "I found it in my bedroom down in Oakland after the cops left."

Millie accepted her intimate apparel without evident embarrassment. "Thanks, Nick. Glad to have it. These are kind of expensive, you know."

"Like how much?" asked François.

"Oh, I don't know. I think this one was $18."

"That's only $9 apiece," he pointed out.

"N-N-Nick!" exclaimed Millie. "I didn't think you were that kind of boy."

"What kind is that?" I asked. We had twisted toward each other on the swings so our knees were almost touching.

"You know. Interested in girls' bodies. I thought all you cared about was English literature and computers. And telling me how great Lefty is."

"I'm interested in you," whispered François, leaning forward. "A lot." Thank God it was dark. I had a T.E. the size of an old-growth redwood.

"Gee, Nick," whispered Millie, also leaning forward. "That's a surprise."

"Is it?" François asked.

Millie didn't answer. Her lips were blocked by François' feverish tongue. While he busied himself, I ruminated on a surprising discovery. Girls' lips were not all the same. Millie's tasted and felt entirely different from Sheeni's. The bold François soon discovered her breasts felt different as well.

"Gee, Nick," said Millie, coming up for air and looking around. "This is kind of exposed. Let's go over there where those trees are."

We crept furtively toward the even blacker shadows under tall fir trees, and lay down on the still warm grass. Within ten seconds, I felt an evening breeze and Millie's warm hand on my cock. I groped for her zipper as François nipped teasingly at her lips. "Be careful of my bruise," she cautioned, as François slipped down her jeans and tugged at her panties. He moved down and probed experimentally with his tongue for her fragrant moistness. Lefty was wrong, realized Nick. It doesn't taste at all like chicken.

Millie groaned, but not from pleasure. "Nick! Watch out for my bruise!"

"Sorry," I replied. It was so dark you couldn't see a vagina in front of your face.

"Here," she said, searching in her purse and taking out a small flashlight, "I'll show you." She shined the beam on a milky white thigh, discolored by a huge purplish-yellow bruise.

Mildly revolted, François moved up to what was probably a pink nipple, as Millie softly stroked the tip of my throbbing T.E.

"Do you have a condom, Nickie?" she asked. (The six most inflammatory words in the English language.)

"Right here," replied François, reaching into his pocket.

Emptiness. Zero. Total void.

Panicky, I felt around in my other pockets.

Desolation. The utter vacuum of space.

"Shit!" whispered François. "It must have fallen out somewhere. I know, I'll just pull out before I come."

"No way, tiger," she replied. "I learned my lesson. Here."

A dozen expert strokes later, Millie had a wet hand. When, some seconds later, I resumed command of my conscious mind, I asked, "What about you?"

"Do me with your tongue," she replied. "But watch out for my bruise."

So François set to work. Millie guided him on target. "Up. Down a little. To the right. There. Oh, yes!" While François labored linguistically, I pondered the flavor question. More like a mushroom and Guyere omelet with a small Greek salad on the side. Nice, but Lefty was right. Your tongue does get tired. Just as I felt the onset of crippling lingual paralysis, Millie shuddered and quaked in great convulsive waves. Wow, girls have orgasms too.

"You do that so well, Nick," said Millie later, as we lay in each other's arms. "And you don't stop to rest. That's nice."

"It comes with experience," replied François, shifting uncomfortably. He didn't like the way Millie was shining her flashlight on his shrunken member.

"There was just one thing I was wondering," she said.

"What's that?" I asked, with some trepidation.

"What were they doing logging in a Boy Scout camp?"

"They were thinning out the trees," I replied. "Too much masturbation in the woods."

When I got home an hour later, Dad was supine on the couch in his usual alcoholic haze.

"Some girl called for you," he slurred.

"Who?" I demanded.

"I don't know. Some funny name. It was long distance. From Santa Cruz."

My One and Only Love! "What did you tell her, Dad?"

"What do you think? I said the stud was out with some babe. Funny, I think I heard her voice somewhere before."

Total scrotum-tingling panic!

SUNDAY, October 7 — 1:15 a.m. After Dad and Lacey finally went to bed, I called Sheeni's number in Santa Cruz. Some girl answered. Speaking French.

"May I speak to Sheeni, please?"

Short Frog speak.

"Sheeni Saunders. She's a student there."

Longer Frog speak. Female tittering in the background.

"I can't understand you. Please speak English. This is important."

More Frog speak.

"I tell you, this is a life or death emergency!"

More Frog speak. More laughing.

"OK. Could you tell her Nick called? Please tell Sheeni to call Nick Twisp first thing in the morning. OK?"

Long, labored Frog speak.

"Oh, go stuff it in your sourcil!" I hissed, slamming down the phone.

10:30 a.m. A long, sleepless night followed by a glum breakfast. I am wracked by guilt. How could I have betrayed Sheeni so wantonly? And why did she have to find out? Even the milk on my Cheerios poured out sour. I ate the repulsive gruel anyway to atone for my treachery. Then the phone rang. Lacey said it was for me.

"Good morning, darling," I said brightly.

"I hate your stinking guts!"

"Lefty, what did I do now, guy?"

"You know what you did, traitor. Millie called me this morning. From soccer camp."

"Oh. She did," I mumbled, shocked. "What, what did she say?"

"She said she made it with you last night!"

"And I suppose you believed her? Lefty, the woman is desperate. She's trying to make you jealous because you've put the moves on Wanda Fletcher. By the way, that was a brilliant ploy on your part. Wanda is really hot."

"Millie said you would deny it. She gave me evidence."

"What evidence?" I asked nervously.

"The mole on your right nut. How did she know about that, traitor?"

"Oh, well . . . Uh, we were talking about birth marks. I happened to mention I had a mole down there. And it's on my left nut."

"You were talking about *your* balls with *my* girlfriend?"

"Not my balls, Lefty, my scrotum. It was all very medical. She's going to be a doctor, you know. Face it, Lefty, in a few years she's going to be handling testicles all day long."

"Then you didn't eat her out? She said you did it very well."

"Total fabrication, Lefty. You know I'm only interested in Sheeni. I *did* see Millie last night. To tell her what a great guy you were!"

"Yeah, that's another thing. If you were going to make up some story about me saving your life, you could've at least warned me in advance. Now she knows it was all a big lie!"

"Sorry, Lefty. I was going to tell you. I had no idea Millie would talk to you so soon. She only called because your strategy was working so well."

"You really think so, Nick?"

"I know it. I could tell she was boiling with jealousy. How's Wanda by the way?"

"Oh, she's OK. She gets on my nerves."

"How so?"

"She's always bugging me to talk about my feelings. Like when I'm trying to get my hand in her blouse. I don't know if I have any feelings. I think I'm too young for that stuff."

"She wants to know if you like her."

"But I don't like her much. She bugs me. I like Millie. I've liked her since I was 10."

"Well, Wanda can probably figure that out. You'll have to do more sincere lying. That's my advice."

"I guess you're right. Did Millie say anything about Clive Bosendorf?"

"Hardly mentioned him. I could tell she doesn't really like the shrimp. I bet if you pounded him she wouldn't even care. In fact, it might go a long way toward correcting your wimp image."

"That's a great idea! Thanks, Nick. We've been best pals for a long time. I knew you wouldn't do anything that rotten to me."

"That's right, Lefty," I lied. "We guys have to stick together."

I belched. It tasted like sour milk and guilt. At least now I don't feel like I've betrayed Sheeni. Unfaithfulness doesn't count when you're only being used by the other person. Just see if I ever give Millie a ride on my Arabian stallion. Still, I am in her debt for broadening my sexual horizons. I might be a certified non-virgin this morning if the fates had not conspired against me.

12:20 p.m. Sheeni just called. Lacey and Dad were out taking Albert into the hills to pee on redwoods, so I was able to accept her collect call.

"Bon jour, Nickie," whispered The Woman of My Dreams.

"Hello, Sheeni darling," I replied. "I can hardly hear you. Is something the matter?"

"I'm calling from the dorm so I have to talk softly. We're not supposed to speak English on campus, even on the phone."

"I know. I had a hell of a time trying to reach you last night."

"Yes, I heard about that this morning. You told Darlene to do something obscene with her eyebrow."

"My French is rather rudimentary," I admitted. "Were you out when I called?"

"Yes. Taggarty and I went to a party."

"Oh, I see. How was it?" I imagined dim rooms full of debauched surfers.

"It was fun. The people here are so interesting. Your father said you were out when I called."

"Yes, I was counseling Lefty's girlfriend Mildred. She happened to be up in this area for a sports camp. They're having a difficult time of it and I think I may have helped."

"That was nice of you. Is she pretty?"

"No, she has a face like a potato," I lied. "But Lefty likes her."

[Page 182, after "death more palatable?"] I just mailed my sister Joanie a belated birthday card. It's three weeks late, but that's what belated means. (You could look it up.) She's probably not home to receive her mail anyway. She's a flight attendant and is always on the road. She only returns to her condo in L.A. to sleep and entertain men without college degrees.

[Page 182, after "dishes as possible."] Mrs. Crampton is mad because Dad dared to suggest she put her obese offspring on a diet. "Dwayno needs . . . to eat good," she retorted. "They want 'em . . . big . . . in the NFL."

Apparently she's expecting Dwayne to buy her a nice house after he signs his multi-million dollar professional football contract. Perhaps someone should mail her an anonymous note informing her that her son is, next to Fuzzy, the most athletically impaired member of his gym period. I wonder how much Dad would pay for that information?

[Page 187, after "Damn!"] Dinner at Vijay's was fabulous: lots of mystery grains, alien vegetables cooked in bizarre sauces, weird flat bread blown up like balloons, and daubs of unidentifiable spicy matter in tiny stainless steel bowls. Piquant, but not too hot for my pallid American palate. Someone forgot the forks, so we ate with our hands. To drink, we had a watery, salty yogurt beverage called lassi, after the famous canine TV star. (Though not, I hope, brewed from dog's milk.)

[Page 187, after "You are too modest."] "Is that name the diminutive form of Nicholas?" inquired Mr. Joshi.

"Yes, sir."

"Then that makes you a practicing Catholic, I suppose?" From his tone, one might have supposed he had just inquired whether I was a practicing pederast. But if he hates Catholics, I thought, why does he send his only daughter to a school run by nuns?

"No, sir. I am a non-practicing Protestant. We tell the census-takers we're Methodists."

"Have you no spiritual life at all?" he demanded, shocked.

"I'm afraid not," I apologized. "Though we do have a Christmas tree every December."

"Your parents should be taken to task," he avowed. "They are neglecting their duties. A child should . . ."

"A child should eat his dinner before it gets cold," interrupted Mrs. Joshi, smiling. "Have another chapati, Nick."

Apurva's mother, to my surprise, was just as animated as her daughter and nearly as beautiful. She insisted I have seconds of everything, and looked genuinely stricken when I obdurately refused a fourth helping of curried moong beans.

[Page 191, after "it was Taggarty's choice."] Since the ladies were forgoing their dorm dinner, they all decided to eat heartily: the greedy Taggarty ordering (in Italian, of course) both the soup and an appetizer, plus the most expensive entree and dessert. Heather made do with a salad, two entrees, and dessert. She's in training and has to keep up her vitality. Sheeni skipped dessert, limiting herself to an appetizer, salad, and entree (an unappetizing grey blob of mystery animal parts passing under the name sweetbreads). Vijay the Vegetarian had the linguini in cream sauce, Fuzzy experimented with the pizza, and I ordered something called grilled polenta, which arrived looking and tasting suspiciously like fried mush. I almost asked the waiter for some maple syrup, but François put his foot down.

[Page 198, after "too much like the homeless."] "In Pune I used to pass hundreds of barefoot and shirtless indigents and never give them a second glance," he confessed. "I never imagined that I myself someday would be experiencing hardships at a similar perceived social stratum. It is quite embarrassing."

[Page 199, after "I'm six feet tall!"] After helping Vijay down the stairs, we dined on Saltines with dill pickle slices and kidney beans out of the can. Not even a warm rootbeer to wash it down with. As we snacked, I called around to see if I could raise bus fare to Ukiah. I dialed the affluent and freely giving Millie Filbert, but her mother said she was out visiting Clive Bosendorf in the hospital.

"Uh, what's the matter with Clive?" I asked, fearing the worst.

"The unfortunate boy has a fractured arm and pelvis," she replied. "One of his school mates went berserk and assaulted him."

Uh-oh. Quickly I dialed Lefty's number. His obnoxious older sister Martha answered.

"My parents are going to get a restraining order against you, Nick Twisp," she announced.

"What did I do now?" I demanded.

"You know what you did. You goaded Lefty into beating up Clive Bosendorf. Now Lefty's in detention and Clive's parents are threatening to sue us for everything we own."

"The cops have got Lefty?" I asked, shocked.

"My mom and dad are bringing him home today. He has to go to juvenile court when Clive gets out of the hospital. Thanks to you!"

"I don't know what untruths Lefty may be spreading," I replied, with innocent calmness. "But I had nothing to do with his coming to blows with Clive. I suggest he call me tomorrow."

"I suggest you resign from the human race, Nick Twisp," she answered. "You are a menace to society." *Click.*

"Are they giving us the bus fare?" asked Fuzzy.

"Er, no," I said. "Looks like we'll have to go to Plan 2."

[Page 199, after "purporting to be her husband."] The elderly radical positioned himself in the driveway to keep a sharp lookout for INS agents while we sneaked our charge through the bushes to the car. He struggled to hide his surprise when Vijay hobbled into view.

"By persecuting homosexuals," observed Mr. Ferguson, "our capitalist rulers divide the working class and pit workers against the intelligentsia. Sexual oppression is one of the oligarchy's most powerful tools in perpetuating its hegemony."

"Sodomy is an abomination that must be punished," replied the refugee with conviction.

Mr. Ferguson looked confused.

"Brainwashed," I explained, pushing Vijay into the back seat. "He's still undergoing doctrinal deprogramming."

However fiery his politics, Mr. Ferguson is all meekness on the highway. At our present rate of speed, we have an ETA of a week from next Thursday.

"Would you like me to drive, Mr. Ferguson?" suggested Fuzzy, tired of watching the telephone poles crawl by.

"How old are you, young man?" he asked.

"Twenty-six."

"Oh. Well, OK. My eyes aren't as sharp as they used to be. Try to keep it under 40."

Fuzzy soon had the ancient four-banger cranked up to top speed—62 miles per hour. It might have reached 65, were it not for the wind drag created by dozens of seditious bumperstickers plastered over the fenders.

Mr. Ferguson turned in his seat and looked back toward Vijay. "And how old are you, lad?" he asked kindly.

"I'm 37," Vijay replied.

"Goodness, I would have placed you still in school," he exclaimed.

"It is my non-Western diet," explained Vijay earnestly. "I eat only whole grains and the pit of the green mango. I also make it a practice to drink a generous cup of my own urine every morning."

"I see," said Mr. Ferguson. "That's a good tip. And may I ask why you wear those shoes?"

"It is to achieve elevation above the soil. Prolonged contact with the earth results in the draining off of vital electrons, leading to the imperfect cell division we know as aging."

"How fascinating," exclaimed our benefactor. "We Westerners have much to learn from the wisdom of the East."

"Perception is the first step toward knowledge," replied the youthful sage. "The mind follows where the chicken pecks, we like to say."

"Exactly so," agreed the radical pensioner, "exactly so."

I nodded off as Vijay and Mr. Ferguson continued their discussion. When I awoke, some time later, night had fallen, and Fuzzy was stopped at a light in downtown Ukiah. Home at last!

"Then why do the elites permit the establishment of universal suffrage?" Vijay was insisting. "Does this not give the masses the power to redistribute wealth through taxation?"

Mr. Ferguson snorted. "Not as long as the rich control the media and the nomination process, and finance the campaigns. Wake up, son. You're a pawn!"

"Perhaps," replied Vijay. "But at least I do not have some ignorant, unwashed, upstart ruffian telling me what I may and may not do, read, and think. That is the world you would create. People do not act according to your enlightened ideals. They are more inclined to destroy than build. A stable society must be structured to suppress man's innate evil. Humans are greedy, envious, covetous, and murderous."

"Well, at least the Republicans are," I observed.

Vijay poked me in the ribs. "You have deafened us with your snoring, Nick! Do not assault us further with your inane opinions!"

"Sheeni is a card-carrying liberal," I taunted.

"She is beautifully misguided," replied Vijay. "I hope someday I shall have an opportunity to change that."

What did he mean by that?

8:10 p.m. We dropped Vijay off first.

"What explanation shall I offer my parents concerning my clothes?" he whispered.

"Say you've been invited to join a fraternity at school," I replied. "Tell them the clothes are part of an initiation ritual. They won't mind. Parents love to think their kids are at the center of the social vortex."

"Good idea. I'll try it."

"Keep a sharp eye out for INS agents, young man," called Mr. Ferguson.

"I will," Vijay answered. "Thank you for your help. I hope my candid expression of contrary beliefs has not offended you."

"Nothing offends me any more, son. Except apathy."

[Page 201, after "MONDAY, October 15."] I decided to stay home from school and my job today to rest up from the rigors of the weekend, duck my recital-anticipating employer, and attend to the needs of Mr. Ferguson. He's presently lying on the living room couch moaning with stomach cramps. He says it may be an allergic reaction to something he consumed this morning. Lacey offered to drive him to a doctor, but he refused politely and went on moaning. I hope he doesn't die, though at his age the prospect of death must loom larger with every miraculous breath—rather like the prospect of getting laid looms in the lives of people my age.

At 8:15 this morning a call came in for me. I knew who it must be.

"Hello," I said, "I suppose you detest my putrid guts."

"That's right," confirmed Lefty. "And I really mean it this time. I'm in the biggest pile of shit of my life, thanks to you."

"Lefty, I told you to rough up Clive a little, not murder him. What did you do, beat him with a two-by-four?"

"I just pushed him down! How was I to know the shrimp's glandular condition gave him brittle bones? His parents oughta make him wear a sign or something. Hey man, I got a glandular condition too."

"And a very important gland it is," I agreed. "Clearly, Lefty, you are not culpable here. Just tell the judge you were playing tackle football and mistakenly thought Clive was in possession of the ball. I'm sure he'll let you off."

"What about the leather jacket and the boombox?"

"Uh, what jacket and boombox?"

Lefty sighed. "The ones I had with me when the cops took me down to juvenile hall. The ones with the price tags still on them that I didn't have no receipts for."

"Oh those," I said. "Damn, they got you for shoplifting too, huh?"

"Grand larceny!" he exclaimed. "Even though the jacket's really cheap leather and the boombox doesn't even have a CD player."

"Did you admit you stole them?"

"No way. You think I'm stupid? I said I found 'em. The cops didn't believe me though."

"OK, Lefty. Here's what you do. You say you felt so guilty about hurting Clive, you didn't want to tell the truth. But now you realize you have to. It was Clive who stole the goods, and you were trying to persuade him to take them back when he accidentally got pushed down."

"Wow, Nick!" exclaimed Lefty. "That is pure genius!"

"You'll have to look sincere. Maybe cry a little. Can you do it?"

"Oh man, I'll put on such an acting job, even Clive'll think he's guilty."

"I know you can do it, Lefty. You're a really talented liar."

"Thanks, Nick. But what if they call Millie as a witness? She knows all about the stuff I've swiped. She could put me away for 20 years."

"You've got to win Millie back over to your side. Fast."

"How do I do that? She spends all her free time at the hospital visiting that faker Bosendorf."

"Millie has a natural affinity for the sick," I observed. "That's why she wants to be an anesthesiologist. To get her back, you simply have to be sicker than Clive. You have to get in the hospital too. Plus, it will give you some valuable sympathy points with the judge."

"But I'm not sick," protested Lefty. "I feel fine."

"Well, haven't your parents been bugging you to get that operation?"

"No way are those doctors going to cut on me down there!" he declared.

"Now's the time for it, Lefty," I insisted. "It's perfect. You'll get everything straightened out—your police record, Clive Bosendorf, Millie Filbert, and your dick. You'll have a completely clean slate."

"You think so, Nick?" said Lefty, starting to waver. "Would you do it? Really?"

"In a flash. As soon as we hang up, grab your crotch and start bellowing. By tonight, I guarantee it, Millie Filbert will be at your bedside feeding you restorative soup."

"Soup makes me pee," he complained. "What if it hurts? What if I get a hard-on from seeing Millie and I start ripping my stitches?"

"The doctors think of all that," I said. "Don't worry!"

"OK, Nick. But if this doesn't work, I am really going to despise you. Our friendship will be over for all time."

"Trust me, Lefty. This plan cannot fail. Plus, think of all the school you'll get to miss."

"Hey, that's true. I got a big chemistry test on Wednesday too. OK, I'll do it!"

[Page 206, after "Mom just got shackled to."] When we got home, a large cardboard box from Sheeni was waiting for me in the middle of the living room. I tried to sneak it into my room, but Dad made me open it right there. Inside was a short mash note and assorted sleeping bags, packs, clothing, and a dog-eared copy of "The Rime of the Ancient Mariner."

"What's all this stuff?" demanded Dad.

"Earthquake relief supplies," I replied. "We're collecting them at school."

"That looks like the jacket I bought you last summer at the flea market," he pointed out.

"No, Dad," I replied. "The jacket you bought was much nicer."

"Well, yeah. I guess it was."

[Page 209, after "Knows How (I hope).] I thanked Sheeni for returning our hastily abandoned belongings.

"My pleasure, Nickie. I was concerned that you all might catch colds without your jackets. The postage came to $12.10."

"Uh, I'll send you a check," I said.

"I'd appreciate it, darling. My inadequate monthly allowance seems to evaporate with remarkable celerity. I am all out of eyeliner and simply can't afford to buy any until Father's next check arrives. You have no idea what a handicap this is. Fortunately, Taggarty is generous about sharing hers."

"But, darling," I protested, "you're so beautiful, you don't have to wear makeup."

"Thank you, Nickie. I appreciate the sentiment, however ill-founded. There are a few girls here who eschew cosmetics, but the effect of practiced rusticity they achieve is not something I wish to emulate. Ours is not a Stone Age culture, after all. And how is my darling dog?"

"Uh, he's fine," I said. "Speaking of Stone Age culture, did you hear the big news? Bruno Modjaleski was arrested!"

[Page 211, after "toward room and board."] Mr. Ferguson was somewhat subdued at dinner. He reported that rumors have been sweeping the picket line that the company may attempt to bring in scabs. To make matters worse, his dentures were giving him trouble.

Fortunately for our house-guest, Mrs. Crampton made salmon croquettes for supper—a dish that could be gummed with comparative ease (except for those excruciating crispy bits).

A momentous day for mail. First, I opened this scented missive:

Dear Nick,

Dearest Lefty asked me to write and let you know he is recovering nicely from his surgery. As you might expect, he is in a great deal of pain, but is bearing it bravely (unlike that big, or should I say, small baby Clive Bosendorf).

I visit Lefty in the hospital as often as I can to help him keep up his spirits. The doctors say that things are healing nicely and that he should come through with all of his faculties intact. Lefty was greatly relieved to hear that, of course. The area is still heavily bandaged and they are giving him drugs to prevent any stimulation from interfering with the healing process.

Lefty is disappointed that he has not yet received a get-well card from you. I trust you will correct this oversight as soon as possible. I am enclosing his hospital address.

I'm sorry things got so far out of hand when I visited you in Ukiah. Nick, I have always liked you as a friend, but I feel I must tell you that my heart belongs to Lefty. Probably it always will. I hope you are not disappointed and will not feel any lesser of me for what happened.

Say hi to Fire Walker for me.

Fondly,

Millie Filbert

P.S. I think it was sweet of you to make up that story about the bulldozer.

Well, I'm happy that everything has worked out for Lefty and Millie. I only hope he is suitably grateful to the resourceful and fast-thinking friend who made it all possible.

Next, I opened this extraordinary note:

[Page 213, after "quest for labor justice."] "That sounds nice," she commented. "I just hope he's careful and doesn't get overexcited at his age. Nickie, could you ask him if he saw anything suspicious in the neighborhood while I was away?"

"OK." I held the receiver against my leg and probed my facial epidermis for nascent zits. After an appropriate interval, I reported,

"No, Mom. Mr. Ferguson says he didn't notice anything out of the ordinary. Nothing at all. In fact, he said it seemed more than usually quiet for this time of year."

"How peculiar," sighed Mom. "Well, I'm sure Lance will get to the bottom of it. He's at work now with his fingerprinting kit. It's quite thrilling to watch." She then chatted on interminably about her wonderful trailer honeymoon in the Nevada desert with just Lance and his sick old mother. Finally, sensing my complete indifference, she stopped.

[Page 213, after "familiar creaking, dusty stairs."] The office was deserted except for a strikingly elegant older woman working on some ledgers in Mr. Preston's office. She greeted me warmly and introduced herself. It was Mrs. Preston, mother of a well-known affected twit, aunt of a despised, cake-eating tennis jock, and wife of a man devoting his life to plywood. Despite these burdens, she radiated a compellingly gracious charm. With her own lovely hands she fixed me a cup of steaming cocoa and interviewed me on company time as if I were Prince Billy Windsor Himself on a royal visit to the hinterlands.

What a handsome, brilliant family. What golden chromosomes! Genes such as theirs should be protected behind glass and heavily insured. Why, I wonder, did Natural Selection progress so forthrightly in their case, yet stagger so drunkenly down a blind alley in the case of the Twisps?

Preoccupied with these imponderables, I set to work arranging the ever-accumulating "P" files in a shiny new plywood filing cabinet.

[Page 218, after "ordering ginger ale."] As the bottle made the rounds, the wine and the conversation mellowed. "You have a tremendous weight bench, Frank," I observed. "Do you aspire to become Mr. Universe?"

"Too much body shaving," replied Fuzzy. "I'm just trying to bulk up for football. It's depressing. I eat like a pig and can't gain an ounce. I just get hairier."

"Puberty will not be denied," slurred Vijay. "It has us in its hot grip."

"Say, want to see my collection of Swedish magazines?" asked Fuzzy. "I found them in Uncle Polly's college trunk."

Fuzzy disappeared again into the gloom and returned with a large stack of glossy, well-thumbed magazines. Inside, handsome, well-endowed Nordic couples in full color were doing far more explicit things to each other than hinted at by the staid men's magazines in my collection.

"These are extremely racy," observed Vijay, slaking with wine his passionate thirst. "Someone must have bribed the censors."

"I don't think they have censorship in Sweden," I said, retrieving the bottle and taking a monumental swig. "They let it all hang out."

"They certainly do," remarked Vijay. "I wish I hung out as prominently as some of these fellows."

Always the proper host, Lefty suggested a circle jerk. Somewhat woozily, we dropped our pants and crouched on our knees in a circle on the mattress, our artillery aimed toward the center. I don't know what Vijay was whining about. In the competition for biggest missile launcher, I was clearly fourth runner-up. Fuzzy placed a Styrofoam cup in the center of the mattress and explained the rules.

"OK. Shoot into the cup. Last guy to come has to swallow it all."

Vijay and I nodded, waiting for the signal.

"One, two, three. *Go!*"

Furiously, we pumped away—faces straining in concentration, eyes darting anxiously from groin to groin, chests heaving, abdomens tensing, three hands feverishly stroking three granite obelisks. Six bobbing testicles disappeared in a blur as the crescendo approached. First, Vijay groaned and blasted, then I popped, then

Fuzzy squealed and fired.

"Fuck!" exclaimed the laggard, as Vijay and I collapsed on the mattress in hysterics.

"It's not fair," complained Fuzzy. "I'm bigger than you shrimps. Mine has farther to go."

"You made up the rules, Frank," I said. "Be a good boy. Take your medicine!"

Fuzzy picked up the cup with distaste, then broke into a smile. "What a bunch of slobs" he said, turning the cup upside down. "We all missed!"

3:30 p.m. As I pedaled my Warthog homeward, wine continued to sluice from my stomach into my bloodstream. Feeling extremely light-headed, I stopped at Flampert's variety store to buy a get-well card for Lefty. After selecting a tasteful card featuring a 500-pound woman squeezed into an abbreviated nurse's uniform, I encountered Sheeni's prodigal brother Paul in the checkout line. He was buying just the essentials: cigarette papers and *TV Guide*.

[Page 227, after "porous in the extreme."] He shuffled into wood shop this morning looking decidedly depressed.

"Would you like me to help you sand your project?" I asked, hoping to cheer him up.

"Drop dead, dweeb," he replied.

"Just asking," I said, edging back to my bench. If he's going to adopt that attitude, he can go up river on the car-theft rap for all I care.

At lunch, Vijay was thrilled to hear of his high score. "Taggarty actually gave me a B!" he exclaimed. (To further the cause of humility in my friends, I had altered his grade slightly.) "That must be in the 90th percentile for her."

"I told you she liked you," said Fuzzy. "Why don't you give her a buzz? I talked to Heath for two hours last night."

"Well, I've thought of calling her, but one fact always restrains me."

"What's that?" asked Fuzzy.

"I dislike her intensely," Vijay replied.

"I thought you liked her," I said, surprised.

"I liked sleeping with her, Nick. That was pleasurable in the extreme. But I found her personality quite repellant."

"I could not agree with you more," I replied, shaking his hand.

"Well, I like everything about Heather," announced Fuzzy.

"Frank, what could you two possibly talk about for 120 minutes?" I asked.

"Phone sex," he replied.

Vijay and I looked at each other. "What's that?" we demanded.

"Well, it's not bad. Heath and I get naked and sort of, you know . . . do it, over the telephone."

"How exactly do you do it?" asked Vijay.

"Well, with words. I say I'm sucking your soft pink you know. And she says she's wrapping her warm, wet lips over the head of my big throbbing you know. It's great. We get really turned on."

Vijay and I exchanged glances of wonderment. "Fuzzy," said Vijay, "this development of yours may have possibilities!"

"It's not real pussy," admitted Fuzzy, "but it's the next best thing."

[Page 230, after "at all costs."] "Good," said Apurva, gathering up her books. "Now, recite for me your favorite poem."

All I could think of was a poem from the fifth grade. I declaimed:

> RAIN
>
> Drops of water fill the sky
>
> Falling hard from up on high;
>
> I ain't been quite this wet
>
> Since I took a bath on a bet.

"What a curious poem," said Apurva. "Who wrote it?"

"I did," I confessed.

"Nick, you are a poet too!" she exclaimed. "Now I am in love with two poets."

"Well, only one," I said, mentally excluding Trent.

"Nick, you are too modest!"

9:30 p.m. Another pleasant evening in the bosom of my family. Lacey is sulking in her bedchamber. Dad is fuming in his bedroom. Mr. Ferguson is soaking his inflamed toe in front of the TV. I am in my room coping with a sudden attack of Persistent Erection Syndrome. I have administered three treatments to my nagging T.E. and each time it springs back for more. I am attributing this sudden libido inflammation to lingering Apurva enchantment in confluence with the full moon. Or perhaps Mrs. Crampton is putting aphrodisiacs in the chicken stew in hopes of prodding Lacey back into Dad's bed.

During dinner Dad hit Lacey with a $45 a month rent increase. He had worked out all the figures on paper based on square footage of occupied floor space and hot water consumption. His girlfriend responded by tossing down her fork and instructing him to do something unpleasant with his calculator, his clipboard, and his modular home.

Just as the shouting was tapering off, the phone rang. Dad took the call and listened with an odd, quizzical expression while the handset squawked nonstop for five minutes. Finally Dad said, "I don't know what you're talking about. Please don't call here again." He slammed down the phone and looked at me accusingly. "You know some girl named Sheeni?"

"I think so," I said noncommittally. "The name sounds familiar."

"That was her father," said Dad. "He was yelling about you corrupting her or something. What's all that about?"

"He's a nut case, Dad. It's a real sad story—in and out of institutions, psychotic episodes, wearing women's clothes. His new medication is working great, but he has bad relapses during full moons."

"Well, stay away from the whole lot of them," instructed Dad. "We don't need any more wackos around here."

You can say that again.

I realize now there is much to be said for parents who are indifferent to your welfare. Sure they don't take much of an interest in you, but they don't snoop too deeply when the shit hits the fan either.

[Page 234, after "He had a point there."] At work, Mr. Rogavere showed me how to put melted wax on the back of type galleys and paste them down on the layout boards. This I found slightly less boring than my usual duties of misfiling and mistyping. Somewhat prone to anal-retentiveness, Mr. Rogavere is obsessed that everything should be aligned and absolutely straight. I, on the other hand, feel some measure of typographical kineticism can only be liberating to the prose.

Miss Pliny told me that Mr. Rogavere bluntly informed his employer this morning that "Log Cabin" would be used in the publication only over his "very dead body." After a heated discussion during which an apricot danish was tossed across the conference room, they agreed to an "experimental use" of the typeface in question for one issue on the Editor's Page only. This page contains Mr. Preston's monthly column, featuring his lively personal views and amusing anecdotes from the world of plywood. Needless to say, it is tedious in the extreme. Further use of novelty typefaces, they have agreed, will depend on the reaction of subscribers.

[Page 236, after "She didn't seem to mind."] 7:30 p.m. More PES problems. I can't believe Trent could be satisfied with just a kiss from Apurva. To me she's the Snack Food Named Desire: one nibble and you crave the entire package.

Lacey was so thrilled to learn of Dad's trip, she was almost nice to him during dinner. Mrs. Crampton made her famous

Mystery Mash—a big mound of mashed potatoes with assorted chopped up leftovers concealed inside. I got the scoop with the sweet pickle—the traditional door prize that entitles its lucky finder to a second dessert. Dwayne was extremely jealous and sulked like a fat, unsportsmanlike child all through the washing up.

To Dad's alarm, Mr. Ferguson's dental apparatus has been restored and he was making up for lost time. Lucky pickle or no, he helped himself to thirds of everything. Mr. Ferguson said his dentist has advised him to stop using his dentures "to pry up railroad spikes."

"How's . . . your toe . . . dear?" asked Mrs. Crampton solicitously.

"It's better since they drained all the pus and mucus out," he replied.

I put down my spoon. My bonus dish of prune whip had lost its appeal.

"How are the boys on the picket line?" asked Lacey.

"Expecting trouble," he said. "Those DeFalco gorillas just came in with the low bid on the cement work for that big sawmill loading dock."

"Will there be violence?" she asked.

"There will if they bring in scabs," he replied.

Damn, and my bedroom window faces the plant. I wonder if the landlord would be amenable to putting in bulletproof glass? Or maybe Dad would like to switch rooms.

[Page 241, after "genetically identical fleas."] The phone rang as we were preparing to sit comatose in front of the TV:

"I hate your slimy guts."

"Hi, Lefty. What's up? Did you get my get-well card?"

"I hate your putrid guts."

"Lefty, what's the matter? Millie said you're healing fine. Did you beat that shoplifting rap?"

"Going to jail is the least of my worries, traitor."

"OK, Lefty. What's bugging you now?"

"They took the bandages off this morning."

"Already, huh? That's a good sign. A very good sign."

"They made me get a hard-on."

"Good. That's progress. How'd you do? Are you straight?"

"I'm straight. Straight as an arrow."

"That's fantastic. Then what's the trouble, dude?"

"I'm three fucking inches shorter!"

I did some quick mental subtraction. Let's see, seven and one-half minus three equals . . . Uh-oh.

"Well, gee, Lefty. That's . . . bad news. Course, you know what they say: size doesn't matter."

"Would you chop off three inches? For $1 million?"

"Well, personally, I wouldn't, but . . ."

"How about for $10 million?" he demanded.

I contemplated life as a well-heeled eunuch. A sumptuous lifestyle to be sure, but what would you do on dates?

"For $10 million, Lefty, I might think seriously about it."

"You might huh? Well, I'm living it right now for free. Or should I say, for $10,000?"

That figure rang an ominous alarm bell in my mind. "What, what do you mean?" I asked nervously.

"You know what I mean. I've had time to think—flat on my back with my mutilated dick in a sling. I figured out what happened to that trailer of your mom's. And that big white Lincoln."

"Lefty, they were stolen!"

"Yeah, by you, traitor. You swiped them while I was upstairs in your room being humiliated by Millie and the cops. You probably planned that too. Admit it. You started that big fire in Berkeley. You're the famous firebug they're calling the 'Griller of the Gourmet Ghetto'."

"Lefty, you're mistaken. I never . . ."

"I got the goods on you, pal. Don't give me any more of your lies. I'm going to turn you in for the reward. Maybe I can use the money for some implants. Maybe I can get fixed up before Millie finds out."

"Oh, don't worry. Millie will find out," I said coolly.

"What do you mean?" he demanded.

"At my arson trial. I'll spill the beans, Lefty. I'll sing like a canary. Oh, you'll have your squealer's money. But your tragic story is going to be headline news. Hell, you might even make *People* magazine. Just think what the kids at school are going to say."

"Nick, you wouldn't do that!"

"Oh, yeah? After you squealed like a rat?"

"I'm not a squealer, Nick. Only you shouldn't have talked me into having that damn operation."

"I'm sorry, Lefty. I truly am. But you have to look on the bright side."

"What fucking bright side?"

"You're still growing, Lefty. Guys don't stop growing until they hit 30. That's why they're always so depressed when that birthday rolls around. OK, so you wind up with ten inches instead of 13. That's not so bad. That's decent. You can still hold up your head in the locker room."

"I did grow over two inches last year," he conceded.

"So you lost a year-and-a-half of pecker progress. Big deal. You got Millie back from Clive didn't you?"

"Yeah, things are great with Millie. But what if she wants to get it on? What if she won't wait four or five years until I get back to normal?"

"Just make sure you keep the lights off. Women are not capable of perceiving physical dimensions without visual clues. Their minds aren't structured for it."

"It's not her mind I'm worried about."

"Don't worry, Lefty. You'll do fine. Just think big."

"Think big," he repeated. "OK, I'll do it, Nick. Gee, that's a relief. I was really worried there for a while."

"Relax, Lefty. Just be thankful you're not crooked any more. Those doctors know what they're doing. They're guys. They wouldn't leave you adrift on a deep river with a short pole."

"The surgeon was a woman, Nick."

"Even more reason for confidence. She's been there. She knows what equipment a guy needs to get the job done."

"You're probably right, Nick. Thanks. I'll keep my lips zipped on the fire."

Whooo. That was a close one. For my sake, I hope his doctors are administering massive doses of testosterone. Maybe he could get Millie to steal him some of Clive Bosendorf's growth hormones.

[Page 244, after "How bourgeois, I thought."] Apurva waited until Vijay had finished the last of his onions rings and then said, "You know, of course, those were fried in beef tallow."

"You lie!" he retorted. "It was vegetable oil. I can tell."

"No, I've eaten here before. I asked the waitress. They use beef tallow for additional flavor."

Vijay turned green. "Why didn't you tell me?" he gasped.

"Must have slipped my mind," said Apurva. "I was distracted by my delicious hamburger."

Vijay groaned. "I have rendered cow juices inside me. I'm going to be sick."

As we were leaving, the cast of "Hay Fever" bustled in on a noisy rush of unspent stage adrenaline. "Hi, Vijay!" shouted the Zit Queen. "Did you see the play? Wasn't it wonderful!"

"Most impressive," said Vijay, turning greener and hurrying out.

In the car Vijay ducked scowling into his back-seat hiding place. "That ugly Janice Griffloch is talking to me more and more," he complained. "What do you suppose this means, Nick?"

"Bad news, Vijay," I replied. "It means she likes you." François shifted ever closer to his date, seriously impairing her ability to the shift the transmission. She didn't seem to mind.

"How dare she be so presumptuous," the voice said. "I have in no way encouraged such forwardness!"

"Vijay, it is time that you paid more attention to girls," said Apurva. "Why don't you invite her out?"

"Janice Griffloch?" asked Vijay. "I should rather open a vein right here."

"Don't feel bad, Vijay," I said. "All the fat, ugly girls like me."

"Well thank you very much," pouted Apurva.

François draped a reassuring arm around his ravishing chauffeurette. "And an occasional beautiful one," he cooed.

A fortuitous red light halted our progress. François took advantage of this opportunity to experiment with an automotive kiss. Apurva tasted of virginal desire and well-done hamburger.

"Nick, can you detect meat on my breath?" she inquired.

"Not at all, my love," François replied. "Just sweet, innocent vegetables."

"I wish you two *were* in love," said Vijay's voice from the rear. "I am certain you would not be nearly so sickeningly nice to each other."

[Page 246, after "elastic in his truss."] When I arrived at the office, I was surprised to discover the full staff at work. Due to the vagaries of the Roman calendar, deadline day for the next issue fell on a Saturday. The dress code had been suspended and everyone was modeling their interpretations of casual weekend wear. Miss Pliny had gone all blue and fuzzy in an angora sweater and matching toreador pants. Mr. Rogavere appeared to be ready to paste up type or dig for clams. Most shocking, Mr. Preston was displaying elderly white executive knees in startling plaid bermuda shorts. I was wearing my usual dress-for-success outfit: tattered jeans and my I'M SINGLE, LET'S MINGLE tee-shirt.

After catching up on my misfiling, I was permitted to do some more free-style paste-up. When he wasn't officiously correcting my column alignment, Mr. Rogavere was excoriating his employer over the photo captions. For typographical balance, our Art Director insists all captions exactly fill the line. He says if *Scientific American* can take the trouble, why can't we? Mr. Preston grumbles, but tries to comply. Thus our captions tend to end abruptly or, more typically, lurch onward in fits of prolixity. An example I noted of the latter tendency: "Large computerized planing mill in Arkansas operates 24 hours a day around the clock (Eastern Standard Time)."

To my surprise, Miss Pliny remains strangely silent about these stylistic outrages. Can it be she finds Mr. Rogavere not entirely unattractive? I would pay in the high one-figures for the full scoop on their respective love lives. Unlike most Ukiahan males, Mr. Rogavere does not drive a pickup truck, own a chainsaw, smoke unfiltered Camels, fart in public, drink until he falls down, or brag about his sexual peccadillos. These qualities make him attractive to a woman of Miss Pliny's breeding, but concomitantly call into question whether there is sufficient overlap in their libidos to hope for love. If Mr. Rogavere fails to notice Miss Pliny in fuzzy tight angora, yet spots a headline .0001 inch out of level, what does this tell us about his world view?

[Page 252, after "just went home crying."] Why is the sight of a beautiful woman in distress such a turn-on? I wanted to kiss away her tears while simultaneously removing her sweater. Is this normal? I wish there were books listing appropriate and inappropriate desires for teenage boys.

There has been a nasty dog mix-up. This was revealed when Apurva stopped by unexpectedly with some vegetarian biscuits for her pet.

"But where is Jean-Paul?" she asked, alarmed.

I pointed to the two canines autographing the left and right front tires of her father's Reliant. "Take your pick," I said.

"But these are not Jean-Paul!" she exclaimed, starting to panic. "What have you done with my dog!"

"Relax," I said. "I know what must have happened. Dwayne wanted Camus. He probably took Jean-Paul home by mistake. No problem. We'll just go over and exchange them."

"I doubt if it was a mistake," grumbled Apurva. "Anyone can see Jean-Paul is much superior to these unfortunate animals."

We leashed the surplus dogs and hurried over to the Crampton's littered bungalow. Sprawled topless on the front stoop was Kamu's portly master, eating a fried salami sandwich. Dwayne waved phlegmatically as we approached. I hoped his pendulous pink nudity did not offend my friend's delicate sensibilities. Jean-Paul, tied by a dirty rope to a dented 1969 Grand Am, barked with excitement as his rightful mistress approached. Apurva cradled him in her arms and kissed his ugly snout.

"Mumfny bojuum," said Dwayne through a large wad of balloon bread and lunchmeat.

Apurva struggled to untie the grimy rope.

Dwayne swallowed hurriedly. "Hey you!" he yelled. "Don't mess with my dog!"

"Dwayne, there's been a mistake," I said. "You didn't take Camus. That's Jean-Paul. I promised I'd keep him for Apurva."

"No way!" said Dwayne, rising and gesticulating with his sandwich. "I know my own dog. That's Kamu."

"It's Jean-Paul!" shouted Apurva. "See, he knows me. Nick, tell him whose dog this is."

"Dwayne, if Apurva says it's her dog, then it's her dog."

Dwayne's rubbery masses of rosy flesh began to redden. "Who says?" he demanded. "She ain't got no rights here. This is my prop'rty. She ain't even 'merican. You guys touch my dog, I'll pound ya. I can too!"

Dwayne clenched an immense pink fist under my nose. This

uncharacteristic belligerence caught me by surprise. I took several steps back.

"Dwayne," I said, deciding to reason with him, "perhaps you have forgotten, but you have not as yet paid one cent for this dog. Therefore, you do not own him. I own him. And as his rightful owner I say you have to exchange him for one of these other nice dogs."

Dwayne stuffed his sandwich into his pants, freeing both hands for flexing. He advanced and displayed two portly fists under my nose.

"Nick, we made a deal for me to buy that dog. You can't repo'pess him unless I get some a'rears on the payments. That's the law. I know 'cause that's why Monkey Wards ain't took Mom's washin' 'chine yet."

I took two steps back. "I don't want to take your dog, Dwayne. I just want to exchange him."

Dwayne took two steps forward. "I don't want'a pound you, Nick. But I will. Now you guys clear out'a here!"

I retreated, Apurva pleaded, but Dwayne remained half-nakedly but wholeheartedly intractable.

On the walk home, I assured Apurva I would soon find a way to reclaim her precious Jean-Paul. "Don't worry," I said. "I have ways of getting around that fat moron."

"Please do it quickly, Nick," she implored, wiping her eyes. "I cannot bear to think of my poor dog living in such squalor!"

[Page 255, after "is a serious offense."] "They are going to let him graduate despite his conviction," observed Vijay. "I hope this ill-considered policy does not inspire any prejudice against Redwood High diplomates by the admissions committee of Stanford University."

"Probably no more than is rightfully merited," I replied.

[Page 258, after "by democratic vote."] Nor is Bruno likely to attain eminence as a furniture maker. Mr. Vilprang gave him a D+ on his maple dry sink. He said the joinery was crude, the shellacking blotched, and the lines of the piece were marred by "excessive sanding." By contrast, my Streamline Moderne napkin holder earned a solidly respectable C. Wrote Mr. Vilprang, "Craftsmanship lacking but novelty design shows promise. Shellac blotched."

I think it may be time for the taxpayers of Mendocino County to spring for some new shop supplies. According to the date on the can, our shellac expired when I was eight years old.

[Page 258, after "skipping off."] "You know, Vijay," commented Fuzzy. "She's really not that bad from the neck down. If this was India, and all the girls were wearing veils, we might be walking around thinking Janice Griffloch was hot stuff."

"That's right," I agreed. "Vijay, what would you do if, on the day of your arranged marriage, you raised the veil to kiss the bride and discovered a major temblor like Janice?"

"In the first place," answered Vijay, "Hindu girls don't wear veils. And you always meet to chat a few times with the girl and her family before you agree to the match. But if that were not the case, I would simply halt the proceedings and demand additional dowry."

"Like how much?" asked Fuzzy.

"Like the territories of Kashmir and half of Pakistan."

[Page 262, after "I haven't a clue."] All the teachers at school were encouraged to show up today in costume; I suppose so they might serve as objects of even more intense student derision than usual. Most, lacking imagination, chose to appear as bums, infants, clowns, witches, or obscure historical figures relating in some tiresome way to that day's curriculum. A few isolated pockets of creativity stood out. Miss Pomdreck looked majestically sequoia-like dressed as a redwood tree, which, I learned subsequently, she has worn every Halloween since 1958—letting the seams out now and again to allow for the growth of the annual rings. The chemistry teacher, Mr. Sneelbris, created a sensation in what everyone took to be an immense condom, but which he insisted was a test tube. Top honors, however, must go to Mr. Vilprang, who taught eight shop classes dressed as a Stanley No. 45 hand plane. The shellacking on the wooden parts, I noted enviously, could not be faulted.

The fun continued at work. Mr. Preston conducted the day's business in a dark brown frock, decorated mysteriously with wide vertical stripes.

"Are you Friar Tuck, sir?" I asked.

"Don't be silly," he replied, offended. "Can't you see? I'm three-quarter inch A-C exterior plywood. See, here's my APA stamp." He pointed to what on any other day of the year would have been regarded as approximately my employer's bottom.

"Oh, yes, sir. Very clever."

Reaching for inspiration deep within Great Literature, Miss Pliny smoldered just below the inflammation point of her typing paper as Nana Macquart, a character of prematurely liberated morals in a revered dirty book by famed-Frog Emile Zola. I hadn't seen a neckline that low since Mom stopped going to Tuesday night potlucks at Parents Without Partners.

Giving fresh encouragement to Miss Pliny's flagging hopes, Mr. Rogavere moseyed about the office in the ruggedly manly regalia of an outlaw motorcyclist. More than one cow had been driven down the Chisholm Trail to drape our Art Director's tall frame in chrome-studded black leather. The codpiece alone must have consumed several premium hides.

At 4:15 lovely Mrs. Preston, disguised as a somewhat over-the-hill ballerina, arrived bearing home-baked cookies and sparkling cider. Work was suspended and we all gathered in the coffee room to munch refreshments and look down Miss Pliny's blouse. Everyone stole a peek, even Mr. Rogavere, who creaked noisily with every leathery movement.

"Why aren't you in costume, Nick?" he asked.

"They didn't let us wear them at school," I explained. "Some football players got rowdy last year and set a kid in a paper chicken suit on fire."

"Oh, yes," said the ballerina, shaking her head. "I remember that unfortunate incident. I hope those boys were punished."

"Yes," I replied, "they were required to play all the remaining games of the season."

"Any news from your father?" asked the plywood panel.

"He is on his way home at last," I announced, beaming with filial insincerity. "How we have all missed him!"

[Page 263, after "playboy on the make."] "Any relation to those DeFalco goons over at the cement plant?" Mr. Ferguson asked Fuzzy, after I made the introductions.

"No," diplomatically lied the hairy maiden.

"Come, Meera," said Vijay to Fuzzy, "let us get some refreshments before the pooper scooper eats them all."

"I'm a candy bar!" growled Dwayne with his mouth full. "Anyways, 'mericans always eat first. 'Cause we're Number One."

"Odd, you look more like number two," observed Vijay, helping himself to one of my famous peanut butter and brown sugar-coated celery sticks.

"How are they, Bina?" asked Fuzzy, fluttering his false eyelashes.

"Not as cloying as they appear," she replied, chewing demurely.

While my guests chatted among themselves, Apurva and I dispensed treats to the few tardy trick-or-treaters still straggling up the drive.

"Have you gotten my dog back from your friend?" whispered the nun.

"He's not my friend, Apurva. And don't worry," I replied, "it will all be taken care of shortly. How is the rumor spreading going?"

"Quite well so far," she whispered. "I wrote the libelous accusation on all the restroom stalls at school today. And felt very guilty about it too. I only pray Sister Brenda never finds out it was me."

"Just one crummy piece of bubblegum?" complained a small furry animal, possibly a gopher.

"Oh, all right!" I said, tossing another treat into his overflowing bag.

"What was that?" he demanded.

"It was an individually wrapped dried prune," I replied. "They're good for you."

"Oh Jesus!" he exclaimed, stomping off.

"Ungrateful rodent!" I shouted after him.

[Page 268, after "too labyrinthine for me."] "No, we're generally quite simpleminded," I replied. "Only our mating rituals are complex. How's the rumor mongering going?"

"Sister Brenda was incensed at school today," whispered Apurva, moving pleasantly closer. "At morning prayers she demanded that the party responsible for defacing the restrooms step forward at once and confess her guilt."

"What happened?"

"No one made a sound. I felt terribly self-conscious, of course. My heart was pounding so, I almost imagined Sister Brenda could hear it across the chapel. Then I remembered it was all for the love of my dear Trent and my resolve stiffened. I did not step forward."

"Good for you," I said.

"Sister Brenda became even angrier and ordered a general locker search. She said that any student found in possession of red marking pens or birth control pills would be expelled from school and punished by God. Thankfully, at that moment, I had neither on my person."

"Did they find anything?" I asked.

"Shocking quantities of cigarettes were uncovered, Nick. I don't understand—can't people read the cancer warnings? Oh, and they found a condom in Molly O'Brien's purse. She claimed she didn't know what it was—or how it got there. I hope they don't expel her."

"Looks like you're in the clear," I said.

"Yes, Nick. I hope you won't think ill of me, but I'm rather enjoying all this bad conduct. I just marked up the library ladies' room and experienced a remarkable illicit thrill doing so. Am I becoming an evil person, do you suppose?"

"I hope so," leered François. "I can think of several more illicit things we could do together."

"Father's right," laughed Apurva. "Nick, you are a very bad influence!"

[Page 280, after "Have a seat, Frank."] Due to the shortage of chairs, we both attempted to sit simultaneously on the bed—causing the back of the trailer to dip suddenly and the front to rise up alarmingly. Fuzzy leaped forward to balance the weight and catch my sliding computer.

"Hey, don't you have any jacks under the frame?" he asked.

"No," I replied, "what jacks?"

Fifteen minutes later my tiny dwelling was almost as level as the homes in which the more fortunate reside.

"Thank you, Frank," I said. "You have introduced new stability into my life. Can I offer you some tea?"

"No, but I'll take some juice."

"I recommend the tea," I replied.

"OK," he shrugged.

[Page 282, after "studying my shoes."] "But we must not forget, sir, that Nicholas himself has been doing quite well," volunteered Miss Pliny, loyally taking my side.

"I hope so," said Mr. Preston, unconvinced. "I've noticed some strange inconsistencies in the files lately."

"It's my dyslexia, sir," I lied. "I sometimes get my alphabet confused."

"Then why did you take a job as a file clerk?" he demanded.

"My father made me," I confessed.

"Just get on with your work," he replied. "And let us have no further mention of your unfortunate father."

"Yes, sir," I mumbled.

[Page 283, after "Right," said Fuzzy.] "Any news?" I asked.

Fuzzy looked around and lowered his voice. "I saw Janice Griffloch sitting outside the principal's office this morning."

"How did she look?" asked Vijay.

"Kinda nervous," replied Fuzzy. "And her makeup was all smeared."

"Like she'd been crying?" I asked.

"Well, not exactly," said Fuzzy. "More like she'd had a bad case of the shakes putting it on."

"Good," said Vijay. "That'll teach her."

"Teach her for what?" I inquired.

"Unprincipled opportunism," he replied. "She just joined the campus Young Republican Club. And volunteered to be on my committee!"

[Page 284, after "most cataclysmic kind."] Janice Griffloch now has the darkest circles under her eyes of anyone I've ever seen not actively fleeing a major famine. I never imagined becoming a Republican could entail so much inner torment. To compound the anguish, Vijay has assigned her the task of organizing a Republican voter registration drive among the unemployed sawmill workers in town.

[Page 285, after "birth control in Ukiah."] Before departing, I went around and shook everyone's hand. Mr. Rogavere wished me well and said I had nearly a natural talent for paste-up. Miss Pliny said with my spelling abilities I was certain to go far in any profession. Mr. Preston said that "considering my parentage" I was "a remarkably presentable young man." I never imagined quitting your job could deliver such a powerful boost to one's self-esteem. What a step toward positive mental health!

[Page 286, after "come down to $475."] When I got home, Dad, Mr. Ferguson, and D——e were arrayed zombie-like in front of the TV, watching cartoons. There they remained until Mrs. Crampton called them in for dinner. After gorging themselves on food and drink, they resumed their accustomed places for further video stimulation.

Taking advantage of their preoccupation, François slipped into my erstwhile bedroom. Following his nose in the darkness, he located D——e's odorous school shoes, pulled back the tongues, and squeezed into each toe a generous dollop of Dentu-Lash, Mr. Ferguson's "miracle formula" denture adhesive.

When François returned to the living room, Dad was chatting with someone on the phone. I couldn't make out exactly what he was saying, but at one point I overheard the word "concrete."

10:20 p.m. A soft knock on my trailer door. My heart leaped! Could it be Apurva so soon? Alas, no. It was just Mrs. Crampton trooping through the rain in an enormous yellow slicker to tell me I had a call. I threw on my robe and finished a surprising second in the 20-yard dash to the back door. For a big woman, Mrs. Crampton possesses blazing speed.

"Nickie, who was that who answered the phone?" It was the Woman Who Commands the Remote Control to My Heart.

"Sheeni, darling, what a pleasant surprise. That was Mrs. Crampton, our housekeeper."

"Are you sure?" asked Sheeni suspiciously. "She has a remark-ably sultry voice for a domestic worker. And what is your housekeeper doing there this time of night?"

"She's living here, now," I explained. "Along with her retarded son and elderly fiance. It's become quite a zoo. My dad lost his job and made me quit mine. I've been ejected from my bedroom and now I'm camping out in a trailer in the back yard."

"That's nice," she replied absently.

[Page 288, after "WEDNESDAY, November 7."] They had to call the fire department to school today. One of the more obese members of my gym class couldn't get his shoes off in the locker room. That will teach the dork not to wear tight loafers without socks. Finally the resourceful fire fighters succeeded in prying him free with the Jaws of Life.

During the tense ordeal, Miss Pomdreck held D——e's hand while pretending to be oblivious to the nudity around her. I have observed she often seems to be bustling through the boys' locker room on one pretext or another. Perhaps she feels adolescent youths in jockstraps are in special need of on-the-spot guidance counseling.

[Page 290, after "and TV evangelists."] Speaking of merchants of death, that stool pigeon D——e ratted on me to his mother about the shoe incident. Fortunately, I had preserved last night's offending dog turd as Exhibit A for the defense. So it was the loathsome stoolie, not I, who wound up getting smacked with the yardstick. Serves him right too. Then Mrs. Crampton unilaterally declared a truce and made us shake on it. I hope I don't get leprosy in that hand.

[Page 292, after "gets to cookin' real nice."] I just had a long phone conversation with Lefty, my post-virginal pal in Oakland. He reports that he has now done it with Millie Filbert seven times.

"How was it?" I asked enviously.

"Great," he replied. "It was worth all the work."

"Does Millie seem, uh, fulfilled?"

"If she's not, she'd doing an incredible job of faking it," he said. "It's better for me too since I swiped a different brand of condoms."

"Do those stay on?" I asked.

"More or less."

"You mean they sometimes come off?"

"Well, once or twice. Hey, what do you want me to do, staple them on?"

"You have to be careful, Lefty. In 18 years that kid is going to ask you for $100,000 for college."

"Hey, I'm careful. And Millie has me taking lots of hot baths and wearing tight pants. She's really into contraception."

"Don't I know it," I replied ruefully.

"What?"

"Uh, Lefty, where are you two performing the act?"

"Millie's bedroom, believe it or not. She talked her parents into signing up for a Tuesday night group-therapy bowling league. It works out great. While they're out discussing their problems and bowling, we're upstairs balling."

"You keeping the lights off?"

"Like Wrigley Field at midnight. Millie thinks it's cute I'm so shy."

"How's your size?"

"It's been slow, Nick. I think I might've creeped up an eighth of an inch. Depends on where I put the ruler. One good thing, I am solid as a rock. I got one hard stubby pecker."

"Good, Lefty. Women put a great premium on the solidity of the erection. And how's your court case coming along, by the way?"

"Oh, I beat that rap."

"You did!" I exclaimed. "How?"

"That wimp Clive Bosendorf's parents chickened out on pressing charges. Then the judge threw out the shoplifting complaint for lack of evidence. Somebody heisted the goods from the police storage locker."

"Lefty, you're in the clear!"

"Don't I know it, Nick," he replied. "I learned my lesson this time."

"What's that, guy?"

"Crime pays!"

[Page 297, after "fall cleaning."] I swept the floor, washed the windows, scrubbed down the walls, scoured the tiny sink, and laundered the diseased sheets. I even dragged out the ancient mattress to "freshen" in the sun—a hygienic practice drilled into me by generations of fastidious Cub Scout camp counselors. I also succeeded in restoring my tiny home to a more or less even keel.

François dismissed my frenetic housekeeping as nothing more than sublimated sexual frustration. He's right, of course, but personally I'd rather have an immaculate trailer than a nervous breakdown.

[Page 299, after "alone on Saturday nights."] "I wasn't alone last Saturday," replied Fuzzy, offended. "I had two hours of hot phone sex with Heather."

I hope all that electronic intercourse doesn't backfire on my friend. He'll be sorry when he grows up and discovers he can't get it on without a handset pressed to his ear.

[Page 307, after "And twirl!"] 4:00 p.m. Too excited to think, read, or concentrate on any meaningful task. So I mowed the yard and bathed all the dogs. Everything must be nice for Sheeni's return. Also took a detailed survey of my zits. Not too bad considering. No more fried foods from now on.

6:45 p.m. Dad is dressing to go out. He had a close call at work today. The mill operator accidentally let fall two tons of gravel just inches from where Dad was unwrapping a cherry cupcake. Dad escaped unscathed, but the cupcake was never found. Uncle Polly stormed up the catwalk and fired the careless operator on the spot. Then Fuzzy's dad immediately reinstated him. So Uncle Polly warned Dad not to loiter under the chutes and to wear his hardhat at all times.

[Page 308, after "want to think about it."] "Frank, I'll keep you posted if there's any action at my end. What are your plans?"

"Calling Heather, Nick. So the line may be busy for a while."

"What's on the agenda for tonight?"

"I was thinking of trying something new. Maybe getting into a threesome with the operator. What do you think, Nick?"

"Just don't melt the phone, Frank."

[Page 313, after "what I'm afraid of."] 4:30 p.m. Too nervous to write. Each time the phone rings I have another debilitating heart seizure. Of course, this *would* be the day every boiler room operation in Northern California calls with news of exciting vinyl siding offers.

Dad just received some bad news from his car insurance agent. He had missed a few too many payments on his policy. It's a good thing he can walk to work.

[Page 315, after "his parole hearing."] Dad is working late at the office—the result of a slight mishap. This afternoon, while he was partaking in a union-sanctioned coffee break (always militantly observed by Twisps), his load matured past the point of no return. When he finally went to discharge it, the tank spun industriously but no concrete emerged. Now Dad is deep inside the steel tank, jack-hammering out nine cubic yards of granite-hard cement. Mrs. Crampton packed his dinner in a basket (padlocked to deter tampering) and gave it to D——e to deliver. She also enclosed the eight aspirin Dad requested.

Mr. Ferguson continues his fetus-like absorption in kiddie TV. Even lethargic D——e is showing signs of restiveness under the nonstop bombardment of animated vacuity interspersed with endless toy commercials. I watched for an hour, hoping the therapeutic media violence would relieve my gnawing anxiety, but had to leave when I found myself commenting out loud on the plot to D——e.

Good thing Dad isn't here.

[Page 315, after "massive sedative overdoses."] Dad is back—monumentally fatigued, powdered like a donut with a fine white dust, and deaf as Quasimodo. Just as he emerged from the shower, Mrs. DeFalco telephoned. Dad kept repeating "Say again," until his caller concluded she was being had and hung up. I hope he hasn't cost both of us a pleasant evening's diversion.

TUESDAY, November 19 — ANOTHER CATACLYSMIC DISASTER! What incredibly bad karma. I must have racked up some record-setting penalty points in my previous lives. Who was I anyway—Adolf Hitler's personal attorney?

[Page 317, after "what is happening."] 9:45 a.m. As I sat by the phone, disconsolately eating a cruller, it rang. Or, for you doctrinaire grammarians: As I, disconsolately eating a cruller, sat by the phone, it rang.

"I hate your slimy guts!" said a familiar voice.

"I'm sorry, Lefty," I replied. "You'll have to wait your turn."

"I hate your putrid guts!"

"Sorry, pal," I said. "My abuse quota is all filled up. I suggest you call back after the new year."

"You're going to be sorry you were ever born!"

"OK, Lefty. It can't wait, huh? What's up now?"

"I had a date last night with Millie."

"I know. It was bowling night. Did you roll any strikes?"

"We went up to her room and turned out all the lights."

"Good work, guy. I wish I could have been there to study your technique."

"Millie had a surprise waiting for me."

"Like what? Spearmint-flavored condoms? Norwegian sex novelties? Edible panties?"

"No, asshole," replied Lefty, "glow in the dark sheets!"

"Oh," I said darkly. "Uh, how bright did they glow?"

"Very bright. She said she got them so she could see my scar. She saw all right!"

"Er, what did she say?" I asked, dreading the reply.

"She said a guy's equipment doesn't keep on growing until he's 30! She said this is all as big as I can expect to get! She says you're a dirty rotten liar!"

"Difference of opinion, Lefty," I replied evenly. "What we've got here are two divergent interpretations of available medical data."

"What we've got here," he replied, "is a traitor who deserves to fry for arson."

"Lefty!" I implored, "you wouldn't do that to a pal!"

"Maybe not," he conceded. "I promised you I wouldn't."

"That's right," I reminded him.

"So I told Millie. She's going to turn you in and we're going to split the $10,000 reward."

"Lefty, you can't do that! I'm in enough trouble here as it is."

"Too bad, back stabber."

"Lefty! Where's Millie now? I need to talk to her."

"Call the Berkeley Police, traitor. That's where she just left for."

"Thanks a pantsfull, pal," I sighed.

"Don't mention it, Nick. And thanks for the $5,000."

"OK. Spend your blood money," I said. "But just remember one thing."

"What's that?" asked Lefty.

"You're still a shrimp."

I won't repeat what Lefty said. It would only further confirm his regrettable paucity of imagination.

[Page 319, after "embarrassed in my entire life."] 5:30 p.m. I just blew $43.27 on two large bouquets of assorted overpriced holiday flowers. I had to sneak them into Little Caesar lest Mrs. Crampton conclude they were for her, setting off another crying jag. I'd put them in water, but they're wrapped in festive, high-priced paper. I am keeping them moist by spritzing them periodically with my deodorant.

[Page 319, after "THURSDAY, November 20."] — Happy Thanksgiving to me. The day has not started well. I awoke to discover that sometime during the night my extortionate bouquets had violently transmogrified. They now resemble some grim floral vestige of a post-holocaust nuclear winter. Oh well, I have no choice. I shall take them anyway. As the Florists Marketing Council reminds us: it's the thought that counts.

[Page 322, after "as usual," she replied.] "Oh, Lacey, what remarkable flowers. I bet Nick brought those!"

"All the flower shops are closed today," I said coldly. "I had to buy them yesterday."

"Well, Mrs. Saunders is certainly enjoying hers," she replied.

Sheeni's mother, now humming softly, had inserted her face deep into her bouquet. The tune I recognized as "Anchors Away." Still studying me intently, Sheeni's father began to whistle along.

"Well, I'd better put these flowers in water," said Lacey. "We'll let Mother Saunders keep hers for the time being."

[Page 322, after "We have cable TV," I said.] The martial humming and whistling grew louder.

"Sheeni's parents are certainly quite musical," observed Taggarty, turning up the volume on her grating voice. "Perhaps we can have a sing-along around the piano later. Isn't that what you people in small, isolated hamlets do in the evenings?"

"When we're not interbreeding," I replied.

[Page 324, after "metallic can coatings."] "Lacey made the soup," announced Paul proudly.

"The instructions said to warm it in a pan, but I microwaved it instead," she noted.

"Delicious," I lied.

"It swims on my tongue, tall youth," said my table companion.

"Yes, sir," I replied, noticing for the first time that my future father-in-law was raising a remarkable crop of white hair in his ears. I pray Sheeni has not inherited this tendency.

[Page 324, after "she whispered coyly."] Mr. Saunders put down his fork and stared intently at my jacket. "Fascinating weave," he remarked.

"Genuine Harris Tweed," I replied. "Hand-woven on the Outer Hebrides—wherever that may be."

"I believe they are small islands off the west coast of Scotland," replied my encyclopedic inamorata.

[Page 331, after "any knowledge of the affair."] 2:30 p.m. Nothing on TV except USC football. I am watching for the sake of my former friend Fuzzy, the aspiring jock whose sexy mother recently tried to seduce me. I wonder if Dad will be asking her out again, despite her husband's lawsuit against him. Dad just left a message for Joanie in which he expressed a desire to strangle me with his bare hands. Maybe Mom informed him she was cutting off my child-support payments. It's a good thing Dad may be going to prison soon for filling his former girlfriend's car with cement. An enforced confinement should give him plenty of time to cool off.

3:30 p.m. Halftime. USC is ahead 62-14. Still the crowd is screaming for more blood. I wonder if Bruno Preston, Sheeni's inaugural lover, is in the stands. Perhaps there will be a stampede and he will be crushed to death. Not likely, given my present string of bad luck. One of the Trojan cheerleaders looks just like my former friend Lefty's treacherous girlfriend Millie Filbert, who ratted on me to collect a $10,000 reward from Berkeley arson investigators. François hates her, but deep-down I wonder if I wouldn't have done the same thing in her place. In these times, who wouldn't betray their friends for a nice cash windfall?

[Page 332, after "messages from my parents?"] On this date they shot Kennedy all those years ago. I think I know now how he must have felt.

[Page 336, after "shorter than my body."] Speaking of acute pain, I wonder where Sheeni is at this moment? I wonder if she is worried how I am getting along in faraway, exotic India? Listen, darling, wherever you are, here is a telepathic love message: "We will be together again. Soon! I shall find a way!"

[Page 337, after "soon to its tyranny."] After breakfast (I found a good donut shop just a block away), I took a stroll around Marina del Rey. Lots of high-priced yachts in the marina, but who let them jam in so many ugly condos? Joanie's building is a particular eyesore. It's a big orange stucco box with fake midget balconies stuck under the windows here and there. The upper floors probably have views of the water, but Joanie's unit looks out on the gray stucco of the condo next door. Oh well, at least the developer probably made a pile and is enjoying an active sex life.

[Page 337, after "worst dread: class warfare."] 7:00 p.m. Joanie came back from a session with her therapist this afternoon feeling a little better. She tore up a Mailgram (from Philip?) without reading it, and took me out to dinner at a Mexican restaurant on the boardwalk in Venice. To the kid's probable relief, she even ate most of her enchilada. But I wonder if the two strawberry margaritas were such a good idea.

Joanie said my mustache makes me look like "some would-be, under-aged gigolo." I'm not sure, but I think I'm flattered. While finishing up my flan (egg custard with a Latin disguise), I heard some men at an adjoining table discussing "residual rights." I think they may be connected in some way with the movie business. Maybe they're high-powered agents. They were certainly chugging down the cocktails like mega-buck deal-makers. Three days in this town and I've yet to spot a single star. I must undertake a pilgrimage soon to Hollywood.

11:30 p.m. No sign of Mario. Like me, Kimberly will be retiring for the night with only the cold embrace of sexual frustration for company. At least she has a comfortable bed. I think I just heard my spine snap.

[Page 341, after "floozie in *Morocco* in 1930."] "Joseph von Sternberg made that picture with Gary Cooper and Marlene Dietrich," she observed, shifting her aged amorphous bulk painfully from the walker to a pink velour recliner facing the largest TV I'd ever seen outside of a pizza parlor.

"Wow, Gary Cooper!" I exclaimed. "Did you get to meet him?"

"Of course," she sniffed. "Frank, you fans don't seem to realize it, but the extras are just as important to a film as the featured players. We provide the context to make the drama believable. Nowadays, the producers try to scrimp and shoot out on the street with nonprofessionals. Hell, half the ninnies in the crowd are looking straight at the camera. There goes your realism right out the window. If we dared look at the camera, we'd have been fired on the spot. Of course, we were professionals. We knew better."

"What was Gary Cooper like?" I asked excitedly.

"He was quite a presentable young man," she replied. "At least back then. All of his teeth were false you know. His toupee cost over $5,000—that was a fortune back then, believe me. The hair, I heard, was gathered strand by strand from one particular family in rural Finland."

"Gary Cooper wore a toupee?" I exclaimed.

"Certainly," she replied. "They had to use a special glue to hold it on during westerns. Made his scalp break out terribly, poor thing."

[Page 341, after "Boy, were my feet killing me."] "Who was your partner?" I asked.

"A fella named Doakes Farley," she said. "He's a good dancer, but he has a bad case of b.o. He's dead now, of course. That's his boyfriend Jim who Evelyn is dancing with. I roomed with her for a while out in the valley before I met my husband Tom."

"Was he an extra too?" I asked.

"No, Tom isn't in the entertainment industry. He's an accountant. He passed on in 1972. Heart attack."

"Boy, Rita Hayworth was certainly beautiful," I observed.

"She wasn't so gorgeous when she was Rita Cansino," Miss Ulansky replied. "They used electrolysis on her to alter her hairline. She looked like a Mexican peasant girl before."

"Wow, you don't say. What was she like?"

Miss Ulansky looked around and lowered her voice. "Obsessed."

"Really?" I gasped.

"Obsessed," she repeated. "That's why Orson had to divorce her. 'Course he is known to be very cerebral. Rita eats like a horse too. She's always had a bad weight problem."

"Uh, Miss Ulansky," I said. "I think they're dead now."

"I know that," she replied, offended. "I still read the trades."

Miss Ulansky, I concluded, preferred a freestyle mix of her tenses. As we watched the rest of the film, she froze the action now and then to identify her extra friends and divulge more of her valuable insider movie lore.

[Page 343, after "an irate townsperson."] Cary played (none too convincingly) a blue-collar labor radical wrongly accused of arson. Perhaps John Garfield had a scheduling conflict that month. After the film Miss Ulansky filled me in on all the inside dope.

"Cary Grant and Ronald Coleman hate each other you know," she said. "They're both English. All the English actors in Hollywood hate each other."

"Why?"

"Because they're rivals for the same parts. Everyone would test for a part and then Leslie Howard would get it. He was especially despised. I've heard rumors his death was not by natural causes."

"Wow," I exclaimed, eager for more.

[Page 343, after "two jockeys at the track."] "What was Jean Arthur like?"

"Vain. Terribly vain. She insists they only shoot her from her left side. Or was it her right side? I forget now. She used to drive the directors crazy. And she is obsessed, of course."

"Really?" I exclaimed. "She didn't give that impression on screen."

"Obsessed," repeated Miss Ulansky. "I can say no more than that."

I wonder if the Hollywood community continues to be plagued by this phenomenon? I must send François there soon to investigate.

[Page 346, after "that traitor Vijay Joshi."] 4:05 p.m. I decided to skip today's movie: *The Philadelphia Story*, starring Cary Grant, Katherine Hepburn, James Stewart, and Bertha Ulansky as a Main Line society matron. I'd seen it before. Besides, I didn't particularly want to learn that Jimmy Stewart was only four-and-a-half feet tall and Katie Hepburn was obsessed with you know what. So I rode the bus (90 minutes each way) across the vast, car-clogged L.A. basin to the magic dream emporium itself: HOLLYWOOD!

What a dump. The entertainment capital of the world, I discovered, looks like Duluth with palm trees. Endless streets of seedy bungalows, cheap motels, and tawdry shops. The sound stages were still there lining Gower Gulch, but now they echoed—not to the cries of "Action," "Cut," "Print it!"—but to the *plonk, plonk, plonk* of yuppies playing racquetball. I did experience one momentary thrill when I happened to look down and discovered, purely by chance, I was standing on the Walk of Fame star for Frank Sinatra. Reverently, I touched the well-trod brass letters, gazed around, and realized the Golden Age was over. As usual, I was 50 years too late. And why were all those tough-looking kids loitering about on street corners? Shouldn't they be in school?

[Page 350, after "bald as a monkey's butt."] "Did Carole Lombard have a bad reputation?" I asked.

"Terrible," confirmed by hostess. "She has the foulest mouth in town. And after she was married to Gable, she had the gall to complain about his performance in the sack. That's being pretty damn particular if you ask me. You know she was married to Powell too."

"Really?" I said. "I didn't know that."

"Oh yeah. For a couple of years. They got divorced about four years before they made that picture."

"That's amazing," I said. "They seemed so loving on the screen."

"Just an act," she replied. "They hated each other."

I tried to imagine Mom and Dad coming together to do a love scene four years after their divorce. Not for $10 million in cash could they make that drama convincing. Of course, Mom is no Carole Lombard. And Dad hardly qualifies for the role of William Powell's toupee attendant.

[Page 353, after "until they are married."] She was right. In fact, thanks to chronic road fatigue and a bad case of twin beds, they didn't seem to spend any nights together after the wedding either. What a tense movie! Lucy and Dezi hauling a block-long trailer through the mud and over the Sierras. It was like one continuous Technicolor anxiety dream. Still, it made me homesick for the cozy comforts of Little Caesar, my erstwhile trailer-home/lovenest in distant Ukiah.

"Was Dezi short?" I asked dutifully, as Miss Ulansky was rewinding.

"Yes, dreadfully," she replied. "Practically a midget. Of course, that doesn't stop him from carrying on. The man is obsessed."

A new development. I hadn't realized male actors were prone to this trait as well.

"Was his wife obsessed too?" I inquired. It seemed to me having that bond in common could bring great stability to a marriage. In fact, I believe this will be the bedrock upon which Sheeni and I construct our happy union.

"They're all obsessed, Nick," Miss Ulansky replied. "Believe me, you don't know the half of it. Now, you take Lucy. That woman saves every penny she's ever made. That's how they bought RKO. She paid for it out of her grocery money. The day they made that deal, this town was in a state of shock. I wish she'd lived a few years longer. With the Japanese over here buying up every studio, Lucy could have quietly purchased Tokyo. Would have served the bastards right."

[Page 353, after "cuddling on the couch."] They were eating with chopsticks out of a Chinese takeout food container. It was fortunate I had accepted Miss Ulansky's offer to share her Meals on Wheels mystery food substances. (She claimed it was Swiss steak; I argued it was loin of pork.)

[Page 353, after "MONDAY, November 30."] — 2:45 a.m. Can't sleep on this killing floor. My body feels like I went skydiving and forgot the parachute. François has put his foot down and refuses to spend another night like this. I'd sneak up on the couch, but Dr. Dinge has removed the cushions to Joanie's bedroom for safekeeping.

8:20 a.m. A miserable morning. Grey and cold. Yes, Los Angeles has winter too—something the Tourist Bureau does its best to conceal. I am writing this in the relative warmth and comfort of the local donut shop. I have just consumed eight large buttermilk bars still warm from the grease. I feel much better—except for a throbbing headache from the sugar rush.

[Page 359, after "closets and drawers."] What a pack rat. I found programs from World War II USO dances at the Ukiah Grange, souvenirs of the 1939 World's Fair (on Treasure Island in San Francisco Bay), old Parchessi sets, bundles of letters in fading blue flowery-script Italian, cardboard pictures of saints lithographed in ethereal colors, an owner's manual for a 1952 Hudson Hornet, bizarre hats and costume jewelry, a dozen pairs of white gloves, ornately engraved United States of America Certificates of Naturalization, ancient cigars, rusty ice-skates, tins full of buttons, strange garter belts, odd medical appliances, and thousands of other fascinating relics of an alien era.

Grandmother DeFalco's tastes in clothes were similarly eccentric.

[Page 360, after "if François has his way."] 10:40 p.m. After dinner (rigatoni with clam sauce, butter lettuce with marinated garbanzo beans, French bread, no wine), I sneaked out the back door, ducked around the padlocked garage (still sheltering a choice low-mileage Falcon), and walked up the dark alley to the street. Pulling up my collar to conceal my face, I strolled south one block, turned the corner, and sauntered toward Sheeni's house. My heart began to beat irregularly as I approached the stately moonlit Victorian. Sheeni's bedroom window was alight! I glanced up as I walked slowly past the wrought iron fence and gate. I saw lace curtains, part of a frilly lampshade, a section of virginal white ceiling, but alas, no sign of the room's lovely occupant. Doubtless she was bent over her books, adding to her already prodigious stores of knowledge.

"I love you, Sheeni," I whispered, as I walked by. *"Je t'aime,"* added François.

Five minutes later, I approached a more imposing brick residence, set back from the street behind a tall, impenetrable hedge. This, according to the Ukiah phone directory, was the privileged home of affected twit Trent Preston and my hostage love child. From somewhere behind the structure rose a chorus of indignant barks. There was no mistaking those particularly grating sonorities. It was Albert and Jean-Paul, yearning to be free.

But how to do the job? The property looked as impregnable as the Kremlin. Even François had to admit his Molotov cocktail proposal would require more study and planning.

"I hate you, Trent," I whispered as I walked by. I can't report what François said. It would be too incriminating should this journal ever fall into the hands of the authorities.

[Page 360, after "deceased elderly Italian widow."] No video games, no racy novels, no billiards, no ping pong, no Danish sex magazines, no VCR, no swimming pool. In short, none of the technological advances devised by man to fill up the countless hours between birth and death. I did find a stack of old 78 RPM records to play on Mrs. DeFalco's Crosley hi-fi/TV console. But how many hours can you spend listening to Nelson Eddy warble "Stout Hearted Men?"

So I watched TV (in fuzzy black and white). I watched Oprah and Phil and Geraldo. I watched cooking shows and game shows. I watched reruns of programs my dad first watched back when he was a bored teenager. I watched commercials for truck-driving schools and welding schools and electronics schools and meat cutting schools and radio announcing schools. (They must imagine their audience is sitting around bored and unemployed.) I watched kiddie cartoons and the CBS evening news. I watched TV until my eyeballs fried and my mind turned to mush. Then I watched TV some more.

[Page 361, after "horny in the extreme."] "Is that true?"

"Nick told you that?" asked Fuzzy, shocked.

"Oh, yes," she replied. "That and more. He said you have a secret stash of dirty magazines over your garage and you invite friends over for orgies of competitive self-abuse."

"I never!" exclaimed Fuzzy.

"Don't lie to me, young man. I know for a fact it's true."

"How?" he demanded.

"I was there," she replied. "I came in second."

[Page 362, after "obscure film personality."] "Who's your father?"

"Another Hollywood great," Carlotta replied. "The late William Powell's personal valet!"

[Page 365, after "8:15 p.m."] I just counted my wad. Carlotta managed to spend nearly $300 today. At this rate, my windfall will be exhausted in less than a week. I am resolved to begin a regimen of strict economy. Tonight for dinner I had reheated Chinese food with garbanzo beans mixed in for supplemental protein. A thrifty, filling meal that left me feeling only moderately suicidal.

Saturday night in front of the TV. I wonder what Sheeni is doing tonight? I wonder if she has a date with someone? I wonder if garbanzo beans are a depressive?

[Page 372, after "to everyone in school."] Dwayne was interested in pursuing the topic further, but at that moment Carlotta was called upon for some extemporaneous autobiographical remarks. She kept them brief. After that, in honor of the anniversary of the Japanese attack on Pearl Harbor, Miss Najflempt showed a boring video on the Burakumen—Japan's oppressed untouchables caste. This "unclean" minority looks, talks, and acts like everyone else. Being a bigot must be a tricky business in Japan.

[Page 377, after "It can wait until tomorrow."] In world cultures class, Dwayne Crampton experimented with new ways to relieve tedium through boorishness. As we viewed a video on the downtrodden but culturally rich indigenous peoples of Bolivia, Dwayne punctuated the action by reaching forward and fiddling with Carlotta's buttons. When that amusement lost its novelty, he began snapping her bra straps. Not wishing to attract undue attention to herself, Carlotta resisted silently with mouthed imprecations and menacing glances.

[Page 378, after "admitted Sheeni modestly."] At that moment, ugly Janice Griffloch approached the Scholarly Elites' table, clearly a serious act of trespass. Time had not tempered the virulence of her acne.

"Vijay's been hurt again," she said accusingly to Sheeni. "He may have a broken arm! It's all your fault!"

"Don't be preposterous, Janice," replied Sheeni indignantly. "I am just as upset about these attacks as you are."

"Liar!" she screamed. "You don't care anything about Vijay. You're just toying with him."

"Perhaps you should go somewhere and calm down," suggested Carlotta.

Janice turned on me angrily. "I'm not talking to you! Who are you anyway, some exchange student from Bulgaria?"

"I am new at this school," replied Carlotta icily. "But I have been here long enough to hear Vijay declare that you are the last person on earth he would ever go out with."

"He never did!"

"Ask him yourself."

"I will!" she said, stomping off.

"What an unhappy girl," said Sheeni. "How unfortunate to like someone when the affection is not returned."

Tell me about it Sheeni!

[Page 382, after "sweat like a pig?'] 9:45 p.m. François is not speaking to me. He is sulking because I continue to veto his plans for liberating Albert, our captive canine love child. Each new scheme he cooks up is, needless to say, more reckless than the last. At this point, I simply can't risk another arrest. Besides, where would I keep the damn ungrateful beast?

[Page 383, after "counseled Carlotta."] "Oh yeah?" said Bruno. "How about when it's third down and goal-to-go?"

"No," replied Carlotta severely.

"OK, say it's the fourth quarter, you're down three points, and it's the championship game?"

"No, Bruno. That is mere sophistry."

"The championship of the world!"

"Not even then!" she retorted, walking away.

Bruno blew a fierce wolf whistle. "Carly!" he called, "I like the way your butt moves when you walk."

What a louse! Carlotta, feeling not unlike a piece of meat, hurried down the alley.

[Page 383, after "curious eyes upon me."] After typing class, I ducked into a bathroom and managed to borrow a spritz of hairspray from a Chicana girl with eight inches of teased hair towering above her plucked eyebrows. This delay cost me the precious desk behind Sheeni's in physics class. I arrived to find it occupied by a much battered Vijay, his left arm nicely confined in a sling and his nose pleasantly buried in a bloody handkerchief. Carlotta sat down in the runners-up seat and smiled warmly at her dearest friend, who, she noticed, was making a polite effort not to stare at my hair.

"Good morning, Carlotta," said Sheeni. "Vijay was just attacked by Janice Griffloch. It's an outrage!"

"That girl is a hysterical ruffian," complained Vijay nasally. "She ought to be expelled."

"It's love, I expect," commiserated Carlotta. "When the love object does not respond, thwarted desires can lead to desperate acts. I've seen it happen before. Often the violence becomes habitual. My advice, Vijay, is to learn karate or withdraw from school."

"I did not ask you for your damn advice!" he sneered.

Despite Vijay's loutish behavior, Sheeni felt a social obligation to keep her oft-postponed luncheon appointment with him. Seething with jealousy, Carlotta dined at noon with Fuzzy as his guest at the Wanna-Be Jocks' table. She chewed her sandwich phlegmatically, and tried to ignore the tête-à-tête across the cafeteria.

"I'm making a nice A-line skirt in sewing class, Frank," I remarked, stirring from my lassitude.

"That's nice, Carlotta," he said. "What color is it?"

"Black."

"Oh."

"If you like, I'll model it for you when it's finished."

"OK, Carlotta. Oh, by the way, how are you coming along with your plan to get your dad to lay off my mom? I know for a fact she hasn't bought a single Christmas present for me yet."

"I'm working on it, Frank," I snapped, cringing as Vijay rested a disgusting mitt on Sheeni's bare arm. Carlotta will just have to get Bruno to break that arm too!

"Not a single present," repeated Fuzzy. "She's too busy sneaking around with your dad, the fat jerk."

Carlotta writhed in her seat. Now Sheeni was resting a delicate arm on Vijay's repellent shoulder.

"Shoot the guy," hissed François. "You know how to get hold of your father's guns, Frank. Plug the sucker."

"But, Carlotta," said Fuzzy, shocked. "He's your dad!"

"OK, then stop complaining and let me handle it."

"Boy, what a grouchy chick," said Fuzzy. "What's the matter, Carlotta? Getting your period?"

"Up yours, sexist pig!"

Distracted by homicidal ruminations, Carlotta later found herself cornered by Miss Pomdreck in a blind corner outside art class.

[Page 385, after "unstinting (for her) in her praise."] "Carlotta, I like what you did with your hair," she exclaimed. "Vijay, doesn't Carlotta look nice today?"

The bruised alien sat in the runner's-up desk and endeavored to cut me dead while responding with polite neutrality to Sheeni's question. Of course, he only succeeded in appearing ridiculous. Carlotta ignored him.

"I should never have had my hair done at Heady Triumphs," sighed Carlotta. "That woman Lacey has some peculiar notions about styling." A bad case of scapegoating, I admit, but Carlotta felt some explanation should be offered for yesterday's aberrant coiffure.

"She's actually the girlfriend of my brother Paul," confided Sheeni. "Remember my roommate Taggarty I was telling you about? Well, after Taggarty threw herself at Trent, I suggested she let Lacey cut her hair. She went back to Santa Cruz in tears, poor thing. I suppose it must be growing out by now."

"Lacey cut my hair once also," interrupted Vijay. "It was that hooligan Nick Twisp's idea. He liked her, you see."

Carlotta glanced over at the traitorous slimebag. "And you didn't find Lacey at all attractive?" she asked icily.

"Not in the slightest," Vijay replied scornfully. Liar! It was all he could do to keep the drool in check.

"How about Taggarty, Vijay?" asked Carlotta pleasantly. "Did you ever get a chance to meet her?"

Vijay shifted uneasily on his bruises. "Only once, briefly," he grunted. "I didn't like her very much."

"Really?" said Sheeni. "I should have thought you did, Vijay. The evidence at the time seemed to point in that direction."

Vijay was about to reply, but fortunately for him Mr. Tratinni rapped for order.

In sewing class, after four failed attempts, Carlotta succeeded in transplanting a zipper into her A-line skirt. To mark the occasion, Mrs. Dergeltry took off her blouse and cute Ambrosia Krinkler removed her dress. The latter exhibited a remarkable pair of sheer bikini panties, which required Carlotta to remain seated at her machine for some time. They appeared, however, to have no noticeable effect on Gary, who roamed about biologically unhindered.

[Page 385, after "was looking for her."] "That's amazing, Carlotta. What other movies has she been in?"

"Oh, well, you name it: *Dr. Strangelove, Cleopatra*—she played Liz Taylor's big sister in that one, *Lawrence of Arabia, Son of Flubber, Harold and Maude, Rebel without a Cause.*"

"Carlotta!" exclaimed Tina, "your mother made a movie with James Dean. Did she know him?"

"Of course, Tina. Mother knew all the greats of Hollywood. Jimmy used to come over to use our pool sometimes when his was being treated for that bad algae inflammation they had back in '55. Of course, that was way before my time. Mother was just a girl then herself."

"I wonder if they had an affair?" whispered Tina, leaning closer and resting a warm hand familiarly on Carlotta's leg. She didn't mind.

"Knowing Mother, Tina, I'd say that was a definite possibility."

"Your mother got it on with lots of movie stars?"

"Everyone did, Tina. It was the winds, you see. Hot, dry winds off the desert. Santa Ana winds we called them. Sweeping down the San Fernando Valley, the desert winds would pick up the scent of orange blossoms and blow a hot, concentrated perfume over the Cahuenga Pass into Hollywood. It drove the actors wild. When conditions got really bad, the studios would have to shut down production. The actors couldn't keep their hands off each other. Expensive costumes would be ripped in frenzies of meteorological desire."

"Oh, my God," said Tina, squeezing my leg. "That's incredible!"

"I believe it was, uh, quite stimulating. Of course, nowadays smog has mostly put an end to that particular problem."

"Who else did your mother have affairs with, Carlotta?"

"Oh, I couldn't possibly tell you that. Mother would be furious. She's always hanging up angrily on the *National Enquirer*. No, Tina, my lips are sealed."

"Please, Carlotta," she implored, tightening her grip. "Off the record?"

"I can only say that they were all major stars—many, in fact, Academy Award winners."

"That's incredible!" repeated Tina, at last releasing Carlotta's leg.

I made a mental note to check later for bruises.

"What was it like, Carlotta, growing up in such a rich cultural scene?"

"Nothing special," sniffed Carlotta. "One gets used to it. You come downstairs in the morning and there's William Holden passed out on the sofa. You don't make a big deal out of it. You fix Bill a bloody mary, tell him you admired his work in *Network*, and hurry off to school. It all seemed quite normal to me."

[Page 407, after "adjusting my brassiere."] 12:45 p.m. I just called Miss Sanders, my old kindergarten teacher in Oakland. Her number was listed—perhaps so concerned parents can reach her any time of the day and night to complain about the progress of their children. As I dialed the number, I was surprised to see my hand was shaking. Like it or not, back when I was learning to take naps on cue, Miss Sanders was extremely hot stuff in my life. I continue to be strongly attracted to women who can read upside down. When she answered, I disguised my voice.

"Hi, Radmilla. This is George Twisp."

"Who?"

"George Twisp. You remember, you taught my son Nick."

"Oh, yeah," she said, holding her enthusiasm in check. "Hello, George. What a surprise. It must be what? Ten years?"

"Oh, not that long, Radmilla. More like nine."

"I'm sorry about your son turning bad, George. I read about him in the papers here. I hope you don't blame me, George. I did all I could for the little squirt."

"Uh, I'm sure you did your best, Radmilla."

"How's your novel coming, George?"

"Great. I'm on page 12."

"You were on page 12 nine years ago!"

"Yes, but I've done some extensive revisions."

"That's nice, George. How's your lovely wife?"

"I got a divorce, Radmilla. We were incompatible."

"Well, you were certainly incompatible with monogamy, George."

"Are you married, Radmilla?"

"I was, George. He was incompatible with monogamy too. I've been divorced now for three years."

"Radmilla, I've never forgotten you!"

"Well, George, I suppose I haven't forgotten you either. I've tried, God knows, but evidently I failed. What's on your mind?"

"Radmilla, have you ever been to Ukiah?"

"I think I stopped there once. I was on a field trip by bus with 32 six-year-olds to tour a sawmill in Willits. It was a mistake, as I recall, a bad one. Why do you ask?"

"Radmilla, I'm living here in Ukiah now."

"Back to the land, huh, George? Odd, you never impressed me as the hippie type."

"It's quite a cosmopolitan city, Radmilla. I think you'd like it here."

"OK, George, what are you selling? Tour packages? Condos? Mountain cabin time-shares?"

"Radmilla, I'm trying to tell you that I still feel deeply for you."

"You do? I didn't know you felt deeply in the first place, George. You never mentioned it at the time."

"Well, I did and I do. Radmilla, do you have any plans for your Christmas vacation?"

"Well, I thought I'd smoke too much and drink more than I should. Why?"

"Radmilla, darling, would you like to come up here and stay with me? We can get to know each other again."

"And I know exactly how you mean, George."

"We, we don't have to sleep together, Radmilla. Not if you don't want to. At least, not right away."

"Thank you for the offer, George. It's by far the best one I've received all morning."

"Then you'll come?"

"No, George. I don't think so."

"Why not?"

"Have you forgotten the incident in the restaurant? I haven't."

Jesus, I wonder what Dad did!

"Er, Radmilla, I'm, uh, sorry about that. I guess I must have been, uh drunk."

"You were plastered, George. But that's no excuse for bestiality."

"No, I suppose not. But Radmilla, let me tell you, I've never forgotten how wrong I was. I've been tormented by the memory of that night for nine long years."

"It was morning, George. We were having breakfast."

"I've never enjoyed my ham and eggs since, Radmilla."

"Uh-huh. Well, George, I have to go. It was nice talking to you."

"Radmilla, please reconsider. We had something precious once. We can have it again."

"I had the chicken pox once too, George. I don't necessarily want it again though. Have a nice holiday, George. I hope they find your kid."

"I'm in the phone book here, Radmilla, if you change your mind. Don't spend Christmas alone!"

"OK, George. If I get desperate, I'll give you a call. Good-bye." *Click.*

Damn, so much for that plan. I never realized Miss Sanders was so steeped in cynicism. She always brought such wholesome enthusiasm to story hour.

[Page 411, after "SUNDAY, December 13."] — As arranged, Fuzzy dropped by early for a morale-boosting breakfast. We both needed it. Over sweet rolls and coffee cake, I told him about the incident with Bruno.

"Wow, Nick," exclaimed Fuzzy, "I can't believe you actually kissed Bruno Modjaleski on the lips!"

"Frank, I had no choice. It was either that or get dragged kicking and screaming into the bedroom."

"You really think Bruno was ready to rape you, Nick?"

"More than ready, Frank. I guess it's true what the feminists say. Any man is capable of rape, given the opportunity."

"Boy, Bruno would have been in for a real surprise if he'd tried it. I'd have paid a hundred bucks to see the expression on his dumb face when he got Carlotta's dress off."

"And I'd have paid a thousand dollars not to," I replied. "I'm sure he would have murdered me."

"Nick, do you have a thousand bucks?"

"Of course not, Frank," I replied hastily. "That was merely a figure of speech."

Fuzzy leaned closer over the table. "So, Nick, what was it like?"

"What?"

"Making out with Bruno."

"Pretty damn revolting, if you must know."

"That is so gross, Nick. But hey, if the dude's set on taking you to the dance, I won't stand in your way."

"Forget it, Frank. You're my insurance policy now. You have to take me. And don't let Bruno try to cut in on us on the dance floor."

"He's a big guy, Nick. How am I going to stop him?"

"Frank, I am relying on you to defend Carlotta's honor. That is your role as a guy."

"Not when I'm taking another guy it's not."

"Carlotta is not a guy."

"Hey, Nick. Wake up! Smell the coffee, dude. I swear you and Carlotta are going off the deep end together. Nick, Carlotta is you. She's not a chick."

"I know that," I replied defensively. "I'm not crazy."

"Good, Nick. Glad to hear it. Sometimes I worry. Sometimes Carlotta seems so real even I forget she's you."

"I have to make Carlotta convincing, Frank. She's all that stands between me and ten years in the custody of the California Youth Authority."

"Don't I know it, Nick. That's why I'm sticking my neck out for you."

"I appreciate it, Frank."

"So how's the plan going, Nick?"

"What plan is that?"

"The most important plan: breaking up my mom and your dad."

"Oh. There's been a minor setback, Frank. Turns out the younger and prettier chick I had lined up for Dad wasn't interested in the job. So, I have to go to Plan Two."

"When does Plan Two kick in, Nick? There's still not single Christmas present for me in Mom's hiding place."

"Soon, Frank."

As soon as I figure out what Plan Two is.

"It'd better, Nick. If Mom waits any more, the stores are going to be all cleaned out. I don't want to get up Christmas morning and find a bunch of pawed over junk."

Which is more than I'll find under my nonexistent tree. That reminds me, I haven't bought Sheeni's present yet.

"Don't worry, Frank," I said reassuringly.

"You're the guy with the worries, Nick."

"Why's that?"

"Bruno. If he ever gets the scoop on Carlotta, he'll know he was making out with a guy. Jocks like him don't laugh that stuff off. You'd be dead meat for sure."

"Well, it was his idea!"

"I don't think he'll see it that way, Nick."

Fuzzy had a point there.

"Well, Bruno's not going to find out," I declared.

"I hope not, Nick. You better pull the blinds down when you take a bath. Just to be on the safe side."

Good advice. It would be just like that no-neck Peeping Tom to start loitering about in the shrubbery.

[Page 413, after "escort's eye level."] 10:12 p.m. Two hours of labored practice and I can now walk slowly almost ten feet in my high heels before falling on my face. God, how will I ever dance in them? Master that, and I'll be ready to join the Flying Wallendas. I wonder how Fuzzy would react if I told him Carlotta was only capable of slow dancing? It's not like I would insist it be cheek-to-cheek.

10:51 p.m. I just heard some rustling noises outside in the bushes. Love-sick Bruno must be on the prowl. I have double-checked all the doors and windows. Every lock is securely bolted;

all blinds are closed against prying eyes. The phone is at hand should I have the need to dial 911. I am going to bed, where I shall not ponder investment alternatives, but shall reflect freely on my impressions of the day. I have several powerful ones in urgent need of vigorous contemplation.

[Page 413, after "cooled his ardor in a hurry."] In sewing class, Mrs. Dergeltry gave Carlotta a C- on my skirt. She said the seams were uneven, the zipper was crooked, and the level of the hem "varied more than three inches across the garment." Well, what does she expect from an amateur? I say if you want a decent skirt, go buy one in a store. It's those ladies in the Hong Kong sweat-shops who really know how to sew. Of course, Gary got an A on his bolero pants, which I dare him to wear to school. One step inside the front doors and he'd be another victim of the whims of fashion.

My next sewing project is a blouse to match my skirt. After anxious contemplation of the pattern, I have concluded it is a technical impossibility. Darts! Buttonholes! Seams that curve! What a nightmare! Why not make a few nice handkerchiefs or a scarf instead? I wonder if it's too late to wrangle a transfer back to woodshop?

[Page 420, after "pay on the installment plan."] Carlotta agreed, but stipulated that button-fumbling and bra-strap snapping must cease.

"Aw, I only do it 'cause I like you," Dwayne complained.

"Well, I don't appreciate it one bit," replied Carlotta. "How would you like it if I snapped your athletic supporter straps?"

Dwayne leered. "Would you really do it, Carlotta? Huh? Huh?"

"Certainly not," she sniffed.

[Page 426, after "suppose I dress like this?"] Even Sheeni took advantage of our friendship to make her own discreet inquiries into Carlotta's parentage.

"My father was Rumanian," Carlotta replied. "With marvelous hands. He wanted to be a concert pianist, but the Depression intervened, so he became a masseur instead. He died when I was a baby."

"I'm sorry, Carlotta," said Sheeni. "What did he die of?"

"Acute liniment poisoning. It was a common occupational hazard at the time."

"So you never really knew him?"

"No, but people tell me I've inherited his touch. Would you like a massage sometime?"

"Possibly," replied Sheeni noncommittally. "We'll see."

Boy, some people charge big money for massages. I can't even give them away.

[Page 435, after "integrity of her corsage."] "Hi, Carlotta," said a voice.

I looked up into a vast cloud of lavender chiffon.

"Sonya, you look great!"

"Carlotta, be honest. Do you think the purple lipstick and eyeshadow was a mistake?"

"Not at all, Sonya. Your imaginative coordination of hues achieves a remarkable chromatic unity. Where's Dwayne?"

"I can't pry the boob away from the refreshment tables. What should I do, Carlotta?"

"Leave it to me. I know how to handle cases like this."

We marched across the floor, turned right at the snow-capped papier-mâché volcano, and entered the luau area. Squeezed into a baby-blue linen suit, Dwayne had stalled beside a large bowl of corn chips and bean dip. "There you are, Dwayne," I said.

"Hi, Carlotta," he replied, bean dip dribbling down his chins, "what's up?"

"Your snack time, Dwayne. Sonya wants this dance."

"I'm still hungry."

"Dance, Dwayne," I said severely. "Or you forfeit all Tijuana entry fees."

"Oh, all right!" he replied testily. "Just don't boss me!"

Dwayne stuffed in a handful of chips for the road, then let Sonya take his hand and lead him away.

[Page 441, after "I'll give it a shot."] "Great!" said Fuzzy, brightening.

"God, it was torture," said Heather, biting into her eggroll.

"What was?" I asked.

"Being in that closet, Carlotta. All your shawls and stuff were tickling me. I thought I was going to jump right out of my skin. And Fuzzy kept poking me."

"Well, you kept making noise," he explained.

"What'd you expect? I was going nuts. I just hope I'm not permanently hyper-ticklish now. Fuzz honey, would you still like me if you could never touch me ever again?"

Fuzzy stopped slurping his soup. "Is that actually possible?" he asked in panic.

"I don't know," said Heather. "Honey, why don't you hurry up and finish. We'll go back to Carlotta's and check it out."

"Well, the library is closed," I pointed out.

"That's OK, Carlotta," said Heather magnanimously. "You can stay in the living room and watch TV."

"No way," said Fuzzy. "She can stay in the bedroom. We'll do it on the couch."

They did too, apparently unhindered by epidermal sensitivity, emotional disquietude, or the guidelines promulgated by sexologists for expected frequency and duration of coitus. Nearly two hours (not that I was listening), and after a carbohydrate-laden meal too. Is that normal?

[Page 441, after "Heather's bus leaves at two."] Downtown was foggily forlorn and deserted. Carlotta bought the Sunday *New York Times* and dropped in at the Greek greasy spoon for a three-egg lamb, spinach, and feta cheese omelet. They do an interesting version encased in buttered filo pastry. Rather rich, but I needed the caloric fortification. I am due in church at ten.

9:10 a.m. Back in my bedroom. There appears to be a pause in the action in the living room. Perhaps they had to give the sterilizer a rest.

[Page 443, after "the fiction-hungry masses."] Needless to say as I sat beside My Love, examining gemstones in the intimate confines of her private bedchamber, my mind soon turned to several semiprecious ornaments of my own. I wished with all my heart I could share them with her, but—through great force of will—stifled the impulse. Self-denial, Carlotta pointed out to God on the walk home. The temptations of flesh successfully resisted once again. Exemplary conduct like this, I feel strongly, surely must be toting me up some points.

[Page 448, after "affections this Christmas?"] That reminds me, what did I get last year? Oh yeah, $10 from Dad and an official Yves "Crotch Jammer" Derbossa hockey stick from Mom. It was all I could do to keep the heart palpitations under control. Oh, and Mom's late boyfriend Jerry gave me a half-empty tube of hair cream that must have been gathering lint in his medicine cabinet since 1956. I used it awhile anyway. I looked like Rudolph Valentino with zits.

[Page 449, after "going out with that boob."] "On the drive home from the dance he passed such a fart I had to get out and walk the last six blocks—in my tight pumps. Thought I was going to die!"

"Well, I warned him to go easy on the bean dip."

[Page 451, after "and on sale too."] Waiting in a long line at the checkstand, I found myself standing behind a small ambulatory circus tent covered with garish yellow roses. I had seen that faded print before.

"Excuse me," Carlotta said, "aren't you the woman who was in the newspaper?"

"Why, yes," replied Mrs. Crampton, flattered to be recognized. "That was . . . little me."

Marriage, I discerned, had not accelerated the pace of her speech.

"Is your new husband still on a hunger strike?" I asked.

"Yes, he is. And I'm . . . so worried. I'm buyin' some . . . peanut brittle . . . to tempt . . . him. I can't . . . resist . . . peanut brittle myself . . . Neither can . . . my boy."

Well, that's two out of three, I thought. "Is there no progress on settling the strike?" I asked.

"No . . . And I think . . . the damn owner . . . ought . . . to be . . . shot."

"You don't really mean that?"

Mrs. Crampton leaned closer. "Right . . . between . . . the eyes . . . *Blam!*"

I wondered if she had recently come into possession of a hot AK-47. "Where are you staying while your husband is in jail?" I asked.

"I got me a job . . . as a domestic," she replied. "But I'm lookin' . . . for a new . . . sit'ation."

"You don't like your present employer?"

"I think . . . he's a bad . . . influence on . . . my boy . . . You see . . . Mr. Twisp is . . . a drinker."

"That's too bad," I said. "You know I might have an opening soon for a housekeeper."

"Really?" she asked, clearly interested.

"Yes, and I'd pay a good salary too. Of course, it wouldn't be live-in."

"That's fine . . . with me . . . I like . . . my privacy . . . So does . . . my boy."

I shuddered. "Yes, I'm sure he does. Well, I'll keep you in mind."

I believe firmly that rich people should not have to cook their own meals and clean their own toilets. That is why humans strive for wealth. These incentives must never be tampered with.

Putting my principles into practice, Carlotta had an early dinner at the Golden Carp. Eschewing economy, I ordered the Supreme Deluxe dinner for one and left Steve a $5 tip. Needless to say, he was flabbergasted.

[Page 457, after " 9:55 p.m."] A police car just drove down the street, but didn't stop. Good to know God is listening to some of my prayers at least. I'm in my jammies and watching *A Christmas Story* on the tube. It's all about this kid back in 1948 who's trying to persuade his reluctant parents to buy him a BB-gun for Christmas. Amusing but dated. Today Junior would be demanding an AK-47 and threatening to have his gang burn down the house or turn little brother into a dope fiend if Santy didn't come across with the weaponry.

Where did all the innocence go? Perhaps it was all those air rifles they sold in the '50s. Kids got a taste for munitions and the arms race was on.

[Page 458, after "December 24 (Christmas Eve)."] — The ringing telephone jarred me awake at 8:07 a.m.

"Hello?" I said thickly.

"Let me speak to Carlotta," said a familiar voice.

"Is that you, Sonya?" asked Carlotta, now awake.

"It's me, girl. Who's that guy that answered? It wasn't Trent was it?"

"Of course not, Sonya. It was, uh, Mother. She has a frog in her throat. Mother, I told you to gargle."

"Oh, Carlotta, I'm so depressed. I made a terrible fool of myself with Trent."

"Yes, Sonya, I heard all about it."

"Carlotta, Trent has another girlfriend! It's not Sheeni, it's not Janice, and it's not you! Who is she?"

"Her name's Apurva. She's Vijay Joshi's sister."

"God, Carlotta, she's gorgeous. I'm so jealous. You should see her body."

Actually, I'd very much like to.

"I heard you fell in a hot tub, Sonya," said Carlotta. "Are you OK?"

"Yeah, I guess so. I'm a little red, that's all. Trent must have panicked when I started screaming and made me take my clothes off. I sure didn't much feel like it with that goddess Apurva standing there."

"I heard up put up a fight."

"God, Carlotta. I'm so embarrassed. I want to crawl into a hole and die. Trent must really hate me now."

"I'm sure he doesn't, Sonya. He understands the kind of effect he has on women. I'm sure he's used to girls getting carried away."

"Carlotta, I was totally out of control. It was like I was in this fever. I hadn't slept for days. I kept walking past his house, over and over again."

"You were obsessed?"

"Right. I was even nasty to you in Flampert's. Sorry, girl."

"No offense, Sonya. I understand how you felt."

"Then I saw him drive out and pick up that gorgeous dark stranger. Something snapped in my brain, Carlotta."

"Well, no harm done. I'm sure Trent forgives you."

"I have to drop out of school, Carlotta. I could never face him again."

"Don't be silly, Sonya. By the time Christmas vacation is over, Trent will have forgotten all about it. Really, don't worry."

"You think so?" she asked doubtfully.

"I know it. Don't worry."

"I could write him an apology and tell him I'll never bother him again."

"That's a good idea."

"What if he blabs it all over school? Carlotta, I would die."

"He won't. Trent isn't like that. He's excessively honorable."

"Maybe you're right. Thanks, Carlotta. I feel a little better now."

"Good. Now, go take a nice bath and have a large cinnamon bun. That's what I do when I'm upset."

"At least I got to be with him with his clothes off," she added. "That's more than I ever really expected."

"Good, Sonya. You're looking on the bright side now. Keep it up."

"It was up when I got there, Carlotta. But then it shrank down pretty fast. It was just like the rubber mannikin doll in health class, only bigger."

"I've got to go, Sonya. Mother wants me to fix her gargle. 'Bye." *Click.*

What a nut case. I should have known from the way she sewed her seams: too obsessively straight, and such orderly, tiny stitches!

[Page 470, after "read her newspaper."] "Nick, it says here there was a woman with your father at the time of the shooting. She was injured slightly by flying glass."

"Yeah? Does it say who she was?"

"Nickie, don't talk with your mouth full. It hurts. Let's see, the female companion was identified as Miss Radmilla Sanders, 38, of Oakland, California."

"My old kindergarten teacher! She must have gotten desperate after all."

"Anyone who dates a Twisp is desperate by definition," said Sheeni, kissing me lasciviously.

[Page 477, after "dinner at the Golden Carp."] We ordered the Deluxe Dinner for two: shrimp chips, potstickers, cashew chicken, Mongolian beef, steamed rice, green tea ice cream, fortune cookies, and tea. A feast for the body (if not the palate) for only $10.95.

To broaden Fuzzy's horizons (and take his mind off his troubles), Carlotta goaded her escort into eating with chopsticks.

[Page 497, after "acclimation queries like this?"] Mrs. Ferguson reports she left a brief letter of resignation on Dad's kitchen table. Her erstwhile employer was still sacked out with my kindergarten teacher.

"I won't be . . . missin' that . . . Miz Sanders," said Mrs. Ferguson. "She was . . . always tryin' . . . to sneak . . . skim milk . . . into my kitchen. . . . I won't . . . have that blue stuff . . . Not in my . . . kitchen!"

[Note: Except in the UK, the European editions of *Youth in Revolt*, published as three separate books, contain the full text of the Aivia Press original.]

Let Us All Write a
Sophisticated Love Scene

Relax. Neither personal sophistication nor adeptness at love-making is required. That is why authors have imaginations. Those unable to stifle their natural prudishness or who intend to write for very young readers (under eight) may skip ahead to next week's lesson, "Let us all write a dramatic catharsis scene."

We begin, as usual, with every writer's best friend conflict:

Enter Dolores, a lovely socialite of maturing ripeness. A glance revealed that she was (a) distraught (b) Latvian (c) nude from the waist up. [The correct answer is (a). The wise writer avoids ethnic stereotypes and too abrupt nudity.]

"Oh, Charles," she exclaimed. "I hate you! I hate you! I hate you!"

Charles, a tall man of immense vitality, looked up and removed his (a) cigar (b) appendix (c) trousers. [Again (a) is correct. Cigars are a symbol of sophistication, since short fiction need not be concerned with long-term consequences such as carcinoma of the lip. Avoid the temptations of (b) magic realism or (c) hasty dis-robing.]

"What is it, dammit?" he replied, exhaling a plume of rum-flavored smoke. "Have you no (a) condoms (b) dental dams (c) shame?" [Although writers must set a responsible example for impressionable readers, such matters as (a) and (b) can be introduced more discreetly later. The correct answer is (c).]

"You cad! You bounder!" she hissed as he rose and embraced her, silencing her protests with (a) R-30 fiberglass insulation (b) precisely out of phase anti-noise (c) his manly lips. [If you answered anything other than (c), please refer to the appendix "Nevil Shute: loves scenes of the professional engineer."]

"Oh, Dolores, why do you torment me so?" he whispered, tenderly sliding his large, coarse hand over (a) her willowy back (b) her taut bodice (c) the Holy Bible. [Yes, (b) is correct and let's not have any arguments.]

"I love you, Charles," she gasped. "And therefore I must (a) destroy you (b) forgive you for seducing Heather (c) submit to your indomitable will." [Not as knotty as you might think. Remember, these people are sophisticated; (a) is correct.]

Releasing her, Charles casually dropped his cigar into Heather's cognac glass. [The alert writer must keep track of all lit smoking devices and adulterers' beverages.] Would she notice the telltale lipstick stains? "You destroyed my career, Dolores. You alienated my friends, you wrecked the Jag. But you won't (a) collect on the insurance (b) get three estimates from approved body shops (c) deny me my marital rights." [All, of course, are wrong. The correct answer is (d) have the satisfaction of seeing me crawl.]

She raked her blood-red nails across (a) the blackboard (b) the damask antimacassar (c) his sullen face. [(C) is preferred, but (b) is acceptable for older readers.]

He grasped her delicate wrists and (a) felt her wildly racing pulse (b) pushed her forcefully down onto the divan (c) recalled Heather's pasty, childlike digits. [Time to get on with it, so (b) is correct.] His famished lips found her (a) hungry mouth (b) greedy tongue (c) rosy nipples. [Take your pick—all will do splendidly.]

"Oh, Charles!" she moaned, both desiring and fearing the passion swelling within (a) her clamoring heart (b) their entwined bodies (c) his gabardine trousers. [No time for squeamishness, (c) it is.] "Charles, you are my poison! Your mouth is like (a) a viper's kiss (b) toxic waste (c) a Roach Motel." [Although (b) and (c) do elaborate on the poison metaphor, the more poetical (a) is preferred.]

"I design monumental skyscrapers, my darling, yet I am powerless against you," he cursed, fumbling for (a) his blueprints for the new mini-mall (b) a condom (c) her secret snaps and laces. [Yes, now we may appropriately introduce (b).] "Oh dear, Dolly, I think I left my you-know-whats in my other pants."

"How tiresome of you, Chuckie," she said, sitting up and straightening her frock. "It's just as well. I'm (a) morally opposed to this sort of tawdry business (b) your own jilted Heather in disguise (c) due at the club in ten minutes." [Within this social milieu, only (c) is possible.]

Charles glanced at his gold tank watch. "I suppose you're meeting (a) that damn gigolo (b) our abandoned child, now a tormented adult (c) that swine your lawyer." [As attorneys and orphans are reliably unromantic, (a) is correct.]

"No, Charles. I have an appointment with Heather. Yes, my dear, I intend to (a) network for mutual career advancement (b) confront her with the evidence of your treachery (c) slip a Mickey into her martini."

This week's assignment: continue from here, selecting from (a), (b), or (c). Please, no satire or lurid writing.

Report to the Commissioner

We the Members of the Investigating Committee would like to begin by expressing our appreciation to the Commissioner and his staff—especially Mr. Finch, who found the wiretap in the coffee urn, and Miss Needham, who sat at her stenography machine throughout the long ordeal of our investigations, never losing her composure despite the bad language and her neuralgia. Also we would like to thank club owner, Mr. Brinkerhoffer, for answering our questions so forthrightly and for removing Mrs. Brinkerhoffer from the room when she became hysterical. Finally, we would like to express our gratitude to those coaches and players on the team who had the maturity to understand that we were not conducting a witch-hunt, but were acting to preserve the dignity and traditions of a great sport and grand pastime. To those four men go our special thanks.

Based on our investigations, we believe we can now reconstruct the series of unfortunate incidents which took place on the field during the fifth inning on July 22. It is not our intention to minimize the severity of these offenses—they were reprehensible and have no place in professional sports. But we feel it is only proper to note for the record the special circumstances which the team found itself in at the commencement of play that day.

As you know it is the nature of competitive sports that in every contest one side must win and one side must lose. Sometimes a team will win more games than it loses, sometimes it will lose more games than it wins, and once in a while it will lose 31 straight games, setting a new major league record in futility. This does not necessarily make the players on that team "losers" even if a photo of the team appears on the cover of a national sports periodical under the headline "Losing Incorporated." A prolonged losing streak *can* be distressing, especially when thirty-five thousand hometown fans show up at the stadium wearing clothespins on their noses. Nor is it pleasant when an opposing team sends in a 37-year-old pitcher to pinch hit and the gimpy veteran powers a rising line drive over the 355 sign, scoring three runs; or when seven minor league players refuse to report to the team, stating they prefer to remain in Double-A ball "where the opportunities for career advancement are better."

Extensive research by sports psychologists has shown that aside from victories, a positive mental outlook is all that really separates "winners" from "losers." Unfortunately, the team allowed its anemic hitting, execrable pitching, inept fielding, and girlish base-running to defuse its will to win. Rather than finding fresh inspiration in each setback, team members gave way to petulance, self-loathing, and mass hysteria.

We know from the videotapes that the fracas in question began when right fielder Murphy dropped a routine pop fly, allowing two runs to score. Although this error was not critical to the outcome of the game—the team being thirteen runs in the hole at this time—it appeared to upset Bixby, the pitcher, who directed a comment at the bungling right fielder. Bixby testified that he merely shouted "words of encouragement," but Murphy contends the comments were "profoundly insulting" to his "manhood, way of life, and grandmother." Incensed by these "unfair criticisms," Murphy threw the ball at the pitcher, striking him in the groin and causing him "intense discomfort and embarrassment on national TV."

While "coming to the aid" of the fallen pitcher, Murphy was

accosted by center fielder Pozinski and "rudely slapped." Pozinski admits "chastising" Murphy, but asserts he did so under "extreme provocation." It seems Pozinski has a skin condition from the fertilizer used on the center field grass and must wipe his hands and "other areas" after every inning with a clean towel. This towel, Pozinski alleges, Murphy used surreptitiously in cleaning mud off his spikes despite continued "expostulations of protest" from the allergic center fielder.

Responding to this assault upon his person, Murphy struck Pozinski in the nose, breaking his "oversize beak" and, Pozinski alleges, "ruining my looks" and "costing me millions in future product endorsements." For his part, Murphy denies using Pozinski's towel—not wishing to be "contaminated by his cooties"—and questions how many companies would hire as their spokesman "a .105 hitter with zits."

After Murphy struck Pozinski, the errant right fielder was "subdued" by players Tompkins, Gomez, and Jackson, during the course of which Murphy was partially disrobed, causing "great distress and confusion" among the female fans in attendance. While attempting to cover Murphy with a section of ground tarp, Manager Granger was punched in the stomach by someone, possibly third-base coach Dooley, causing him to swallow a "heavy, chrome-plated" police whistle. Manager Granger subsequently underwent abdominal surgery for removal of the whistle and is no longer in baseball. Coach Dooley himself sustained numerous lacerations and a concussion from the "forceful impact of his head" with a bat wielded by media personality and team publicist Melanie Baker. Ms. Baker, who has been linked romantically with right fielder Murphy, testified she "saw red" and "lost her head" when it appeared "her man" was in danger.

At this point the Donnybrook became general and it is impossible to know for certain who did what to whom and how much of it was in the region of the groin. We do know several players received black eyes, Trainer Panetta lost part of an ear and his St. Christopher medal, and third-baseman Collins was "forced to ingest" the business end of an athletic supporter. This last act we find especially distasteful.

Violence, except as required in the course of the game, has no place in competitive sports. Fighting is especially objectionable when, as in this case, so much of it took the form of biting and pinching. The image of baseball can only suffer if such acts are tolerated. The guilty must be punished. Therefore, Mr. Commissioner, it is our recommendation that the suspended coaches and players be recalled from their homes and be compelled to finish out the balance of the season—no matter how distasteful this may be for them. As our old coach used to say, "Strike a man and you make him smart, humble him and you make him wise."

Yours for a better baseball,
THE COMMITTEE.

The Visitation

I shall never forget the evening when the alien came. It was just after sunset and I was out in the garden pollinating a lovely but evanescent variety of geranium developed by my father during the great war. From a nearby nest hidden among the leafy boughs of a *rhipsalidopsis gaerneri* a double-breasted cassock chirped a sleepy tale of bird-woe, tinting the misty twilight with the scent of happy melancholy. My mind, like that lugubrious bird's, was occupied with distant thoughts. I was ruminating, as I often do, on the theological consequences of the Avignon Papacy, when suddenly I became aware of a harsh, whirling sound above my head. Directing my gaze skyward, I espied a luminous, silvery disk hovering in the air above the gazebo. As I watched, greatly agitated, a shaft of light descended from the disk and a tall humanlike figure materialized on the garden path not five paces from where I was standing. It was then that I realized that it was my honor and privilege to receive a visitation from a representative of an alien world.

"Good evening," I said in a firm voice, "I am Hargreave, Geoffrey Hargreave, a citizen of the planet Earth."

"Uh, good evening," replied the alien. He spoke in the flat, colorless accents of the American Middle West. "Tell me, Bud. Is this by any chance California?"

"No, thank God, it is not," I replied. "California lies approximately seven thousand earth-miles west of here."

The alien frowned. "Damn apprentice navigator. I'll have his zipcon shield for this. Well, thanks, neighbor, and pardon the intrusion." The alien turned as if to go.

"Oh please!" I exclaimed. "Do stay, won't you? I should so enjoy the opportunity of discussing with you our respective cultures."

The alien frowned again. His gaze darted from my face to the geranium clutched forgotten in my right hand.

Quickly I released the flower, crushing it under my boot. "I have no weapons," I said. "I mean you no harm."

The alien scrutinized my visage for several seconds before replying. "Little rough on the indigenous vegetation aren't you, Pop? Sure, I'll stick around and rap for a while if you want." The alien removed a small metallic object from a pocket and spoke into it. "Breaker Two to Big Tamale. I've got an inquisitive native here. Request permission for a Code Twelve. Over."

From the object came the sound of static and then a garbled voice. "Big Tamale to Breaker Two. Permission granted. Keep it short. Over."

The alien winked at me and spoke again into the object. "Roger, Big Tamale. Over and out."

"With that device you communicate with your fellow life forms aboard your intergalactic space vessel?" I inquired.

"Right," replied the alien. "It's called a walkie-talkie. Runs on batteries. We picked it up last week in Taiwan. Got a whole case of them to take home."

"And where is home?" I asked, feigning nonchalance.

"Oh, excuse me," said the alien. "I guess I haven't introduced myself. I am Ybock of the planet Zindau, orbiting the star Mithridia, in the galaxy, 12-317x."

"Ah, yes. I know it well," I replied, thinking back to my college astronomy. "Your planet has, I believe, three moons—Zummo,

Zullu, and Zippo."

"Hey, that's right," replied the alien, smiling. "Say, you're OK."

I was at once charmed by the creature's ingratiating manner, and to my surprise, felt completely at ease in his presence. "Would you care to sit down?" I inquired.

"That would be nice," he replied.

We made our way silently up the path to the terrace and settled into a settee constructed of magnificent elephant tusks acquired on safari by my late uncle years ago. Neither of us spoke, preferring to concentrate our faculties on studying each other's curious form.

The alien was garbed in a loose-fitting jacket, lime-green in color, constructed of a light, open-weave fabric of apparent industrial manufacture. The oversize lapels partially concealed two large flaps which buttoned over the breast pockets. The trousers were tailored of the same fabric and flared peculiarly at the cuff. Under his jacket the alien wore a bright yellow blouse open at the neck, exposing a hirsute chest. His midriff was girdled by a white, leather-like strap, resembling a belt. His shoes—lace-less—were fabricated of the same material. The alien was deeply tanned and appeared to be wearing a toupee. His features were average, although there was a peculiar set to his mouth which placed one in mind of Donald Nixon, the late American president's brother.

The alien swept the terrace with his piercing blue eyes and then spoke. "Swell yard you got here, Mr. Hargreave. Mind if I take a few pictures?"

"Not at all, Ybock," I replied, "you would honor me."

"Thanks," said the alien, extracting another small metallic object from a pocket. "The old lady, she'll get a kick out of seeing these flowers. She's into gardening, too." With that, the alien pointed the object at my spathiphyllum—then in flower—and pushed a button. The object made a clicking sound.

"You know, Ybock," I observed, "our culture has developed

apparatus similar to your instrument producing what we term a photograph. By what names does your culture call that device?"

The alien paused and looked at me uncertainly. "This here? We call this a camera. Picked it up last week in Tokyo. Produces what we term a snapshot."

"I see," I said, feeling my face flush deep crimson. "Your culture, Ybock, seems to adopt the products of alien technologies with remarkable celerity."

The alien fiddled with his camera. "What? Oh, yeah. Well, that's how you get ahead in this man's universe. Say, how about letting me snap a couple of quick ones of you?"

"Oh, well, I don't. . ."

"Aw, come on," implored the alien. "Just one—for my son Clint."

"Oh, well. If you insist," I said. I sat erect on the settee as the alien searched for the most pleasing composition. "So you are a father, Ybock," I said, trying not to move my lips. "How old is your son?"

"Clint? He's, let's see, twenty-six zimdons—about eight earth years."

"I suppose he wants to be a cosmonaut like his father?"

There was a brilliant flash as the shutter clicked. "Are you kidding?" replied the alien, returning the camera to his pocket. "Kid wants to be a country and western disc jockey. Got a terrific crush on the Dixie Chicks. It'll be my hide if I return home without their autographs, believe me." The alien looked up at his space vessel still glowing in the deepening dusk above the gazebo. "If that twit can find Nashville, which I doubt." The alien shrugged and cleared his throat.

It was then that I became conscious of a dryness in my own throat.

"Forgive my manners, dear friend!" I exclaimed. "Would you care for a cup of tea? I have some delicious Kinstani, smuggled over the Khyber Pass by a brave classmate of mine, now deceased. Or perhaps, some caviar? It is my privilege to possess a small quantity of Russian ochre—a variety brought across the Black Sea by scuba diver."

The alien smiled. "Say, that sounds swell, Mr. Hargreave. But to tell you the truth the snack items I'm most anxious to experience on your planet are what your culture calls Coca-Cola and Cheezits. We tried to get some yesterday in Albania, but they were be fresh out."

"I see," I said, endeavoring to suppress a shudder. "Well, let me see what I can do." As the butler was ill with the gout, I excused myself and walked briskly to the pantry, where to my surprise I located a small cache of the requested comestibles evidently left behind by the former Mrs. Hargreave, a rustic poetess with exotic appetites.

The alien smiled with nervous anticipation when I returned with the tray. "Please, my friend, don't get up," I said, offering my guest a glass of cola. He held the crystal goblet with both hands and examined its contents with what may have been scientific curiosity, but appeared to me to be rapture. "I've put an ice cube in it," I said, "as they do in America."

The alien smiled. I was startled to observe that his hands were shaking. "You don't know how long," he began, "how long . . ." His voice broke off as he raised the glass to his lips and gulped the effervescent liquid. Trickles of cola ran down his chin as the alien flung back his head and sucked deep draughts of the syrupy fluid. When he had drained the glass he returned it reluctantly to the tray, his face contorted into a hideous mask of exaltation, his unseeing eyes fixed on the ice cube lying naked in the bottom of the glass.

"Cheezit?" I asked, offering him the plate of crackers. The alien looked up at me and wiped his mouth with his sleeve. A deep rumbling emanated from within him and he emitted several rapid exhalations I took for belches.

"It was even more delicious than we had imagined," said the alien. "It is true—the tiny bubbles do create a most enjoyable stinging sensation in the thyductile tubes. Our scientists had said it was not possible." He looked with alarm at the plate of crackers. "But where are the garnishments—the cream cheese with chopped olive, the deviled ham, the pickled cocktail onions? These are not Cheezits!"

Much embarrassed, I apologized for the meagerness of the hors d'oeuvres and endeavored to assure the alien that the biscuit was often consumed unadorned with no diminution of enjoyment. He reluctantly consented to nibble a corner of one cracker.

"A bit dry," he said at last, glancing covetously at my still untouched beverage.

"Here," I said, handing him my cola. "I'm not very thirsty." The alien did not demur. He accepted the glass and imbibed its sugary contents in seven eager swallows. As we both waited for the carbon dioxide to emerge from the alien's thyductile tubes, I wrestled with scores of questions teeming in my brain. Where does one begin!

"Tell me, Ybock," I began, when the rumblings had ceased, "how is it that you speak our language so fluently?"

The alien nibbled another corner off the Cheezit, frowned, then replaced the cracker on the dish. "That's easy," he said, "for the past thirty-five earth-years we have monitored your television transmissions."

"I say, how extraordinary!" I exclaimed. "That these frivolous transmissions should traverse the vast empty reaches of space to be intercepted and observed by a superior culture. You must be tremendously amused by the fatuity of our broadcasts."

"Right," replied the alien, "we do enjoy the comedies. But we are a dynamic race and so find the action programs even more appealing." He paused to pluck a bit of biscuit from beneath a molar. "Of course, it was a tremendous challenge for our scientific community," he continued. "Color did not come on line until eighty-four and there are still several isolated settlements in the polar regions of Zindau without receivers." The alien shook his head sadly, then brightened. "But they should have cable in a few zimdons."

"I see," I said. My throat suddenly felt very dry and I wished I had not been so generous with my beverage. "Tell me, Ybock," I began again, "why have you—you and your colleagues—made this long, and I am sure, arduous journey to our world? What is it you desire?"

The alien looked away and shifted uncomfortably in his seat. Doubtless he was uncertain whether he should entrust to this earth-being the secret of their great mission. At last he gazed directly into my eyes and spoke. "We have been sent to seek an accommodation with your world."

Unflinching, I returned his gaze. "What is the nature of the accommodation you seek?" I asked.

The alien coughed and looked up at the stars now beginning to twinkle in the night sky. I wondered if he was searching for the galaxy where his loved ones impatiently awaited his return. "You must understand," he said at last, "our people are very restless. They have many desires. Through great effort we have met some of these desires. My people now enjoy spotless restrooms, their clothing is sparkling clean and free of unsightly stains, their bodies do not emit unpleasant odors, they experience fast relief from headache pain."

"I see," I said softly.

"But there is one desire we cannot meet alone. We need the assistance of your world. That is why we are going to California. We have been sent to obtain the one thing that will make my people happy."

"And what is that?" I asked, not without some apprehension.

"I believe you call it a 'Nielsen rating box'." The alien appeared relieved that the words finally were spoken. "It is not easy to gaze upon your favorites season after season and then experience the torment of cancellations. My people are a peaceful race. Yet twice in the last five seasons great civil disruptions have swept our planet when favorite programs have been axed."

I was confused. "But how would this Nielsen box as you call it help?"

The alien sighed and began to drum the fingers of his left hand against the arm of the settee. "It would help," he said petulantly, "by correcting the gross inaccuracies in your present method of gauging the popularity of programs. There are more than two billion Zindauians, all avid television watchers, whose viewing preferences are not now being sampled by the Nielsen Company. This has led to unbelievable distortions in the ratings of your television programs. We wish to correct this problem by obtaining a certain number of Nielsen boxes—we're not insisting on equal representation you understand—we just want a fair input into the rating system." The alien had grown quite belligerent. "Or don't our opinions count for anything?"

I endeavored to assure the alien that their opinions—on any subject—would be of immense interest to our planet.

The alien seemed relieved. "You really think so?" he asked. "Say, that's swell."

"But surely, Ybock," I said, "you must realize that your visit—this epochal contact between two worlds—can have an impact far more sweeping and momentous than the mere reordering of a television poll?"

"That's all we seek," declared the alien.

I was shocked to my marrow. "But Ybock," I said, "think of the opportunity this visit affords us for the exchange of knowledge and technology, for the enrichment of philosophy, for the augmentation of our literature and art, for the enlivening of our social intercourse."

The alien blushed. "Sorry, not interested," he said.

I sat back in the settee dumbfounded.

The alien rose. "Well, gotta go," he said. "We're due in California tomorrow. If we finish early we get to go to Disneyland." The alien looked down at me uneasily. With much effort I rose to my feet.

"Don't take it so hard, Mr. Hargreave," he said, placing his arm around my shoulder. "Listen, if the deal with the Nielsen boxes works out, we may be back to discuss a big technological problem with your scientists."

I was cheered by this welcome news. "And what is that?" I asked. "If, of course, you are at liberty to divulge it."

"Don't see why not," said the alien, signaling to the space vessel with two small flags. "We've been seeking the most efficient means of transporting massive amounts of cargo through intergalactic space."

"Then you wish to commence trade!" I exclaimed.

"Not exactly," replied the alien. "At the central post office in Zinduk—that's our capital city—they've got three hundred and twelve thousand sacks of fan mail. We'd sure like to deliver them."

With those words the alien suddenly dematerialized. A moment later the space vessel rose into the sky and hurtled off in the direction of California. When it was gone, I walked into my house and proceeded to get quite drunk.

Alumni Notes

1918 – The college's oldest alumnus, Wallace Gibson, choked to death on a kidney bean at his home in Canton on February 3. His widow Harriet notes sadly, "Wally never liked kidney beans. He was eating them on doctor's orders."

1920 – Famed pioneer aviator, Morris "Buzzard" Nesbitt, died last July 4 when a cherry bomb went off while he was shaving. Buzz was the first person to fly the Atlantic blindfolded with one hand tied behind his back, a feat he accomplished in 1938 to settle a tavern wager.

1926 – Frederick Osborne has fathered his first child, a daughter, at the age of 96. Fred attributes his remarkable potency to "a sensible diet, vigorous exercise, and 95 years of celibacy."

1927 – The college regrets it must cancel the Seventy-fifth Reunion planned for commencement next spring as it appears all members of this class are deceased or institutionalized. Should this not be the case, the festivities will proceed as planned.

1931 – Richard Littlefield died March 4 in Trenton following a long illness. A note in this space some years ago reporting Captain Littlefield's death in the Battle of the Bulge evidently was in error. The editors regret any confusion this may have caused among Dick's friend and classmates.

1934 – Sanders Prabert has retired from the faculty of Chamber's Boys Academy following a misunderstanding over some photographs taken at a Hygiene Club picnic and subsequently distributed over the Internet. Sandy taught health at the school for 46 years and is the author of *Enjoy Your Puberty*.

1935 – William Fletcher writes to correct a note which appeared here last month. He has not been awarded the Nobel Prize for Literature. The telegram was a hoax perpetuated by the "wags of Dimly Hall." President Peabody requests that in the future alumni refrain from such pranks. The college incurred considerable expense in canceling the banquet, states Dr. Peabody, and was profoundly embarrassed by the "hysterical reactions" of certain television commentators.

1938 – Chester Norris has recovered from amnesia and is back with his family in Hartford. He requests that friend and classmates with knowledge of his past activities write or call him. He is seeking information for the years 1947 through 2001. During that time he may have been known as Raoul "Bugsie" Mahoney and may have been involved in some aspect of horse racing.

1941 – Samuel Truett has retired from the ministry after more than 50 years in service to God. Sam reports that his faith has begun to waver and he would like to hear from classmates who have experienced divine revelations. So would we—such experiences always merit a note to your alumni magazine.

1942 – Baxter Hoffman died of leukemia at his home in Livermore, California on January 12. A renowned physicist, Baxie worked on the little-known Brooklyn Project during World War II, and devoted much of his life to researching plutonium decontamination. Following the funeral, Baxie's remains were interred in an underground cavern near Yucca Flats, Nevada, where they will be kept for the next 160,000 years.

1944 – Army Private Albert Keller has been reunited with his family after spending the past 56 years hiding in the forest outside Dusseldorf, Germany. Al became separated from his unit while on latrine duty in 1945 and somehow failed to learn the outcome of the war. "I was afraid the Krauts had licked us," writes Al, "what with all the new shops and supermarkets and fancy BMWs they were driving." Al is happy to be home and pleased by our victory in the war. "I'm glad we beat those bastards," he notes. "I'd go again if my country called."

1951 – Curtis McCrae was kidnaped April 22 from his frozen yogurt stand on the third level of the Dixie Mall in Mobile, Alabama. Curt's classmates have organized an ad hoc committee and hope to raise $2,500 toward the $1 million ransom demanded by the kidnappers. Pledges should be sent to class secretary Tip Taylor, but *not* in the little green envelopes provided for donations to the college. Sorry, these contributions are not tax deductible and do not count in the competition among the classes for the President's Golden Garter.

1954 – David Johnstone, Ph.D., Postal University of Idaho, has been named Chairman of the Department of History and Rural Thought at Cactus Junior College, Del Lizard, Texas. At the annual convention of the Association of Rural Educators (A.R.ED.), held recently in Elko, Dr. Dave won second prize and a back massage for his paper entitled, "Existentialism: A Common Sense Approach."

1961 – On March 24 boatbuilder Ernest Knodlime inadvertently fiberglassed himself to the port garboard seam of the Dixie Lady, a 17-meter sloop in dry-dock in Virginia Beach. Thus far all effort to free Ernie from his plastic cocoon have failed and—as of this writing—he continues to receive nourishment, world news, and his e-mail through a tube.

1964 – Jeffrey Horgan reports he has been cuckolded by his lovely wife Edna (B.A., Swarthmore). "I never suspected a thing," writes Jeff. "It had been going on for years right under my nose. The guy was her weaving instructor—a little wimp of a fellow with glasses, a lisp, and lint in his ears. She felt sorry for him." Jeff has forgiven his wife, and they are presently redecorating their home in entirely man-made fibers.

1968 – Crandle Holmes reports he has lost his business (personalized cupcakes via the Internet) and is living in a camper at a reststop on Interstate 95. "Where were all my hotshot friends when I needed them?" he writes.

1969 – Michael Oster's request for a parole or more toilet paper has again been denied by state prison authorities. Mike is serving a 40-years-to-life sentence for crimes committed during the occupation of Dimly Hall by SDS members protesting the war in Vietnam. Throughout his long prison confinement, Mike has steadfastly denied that he was the student radical who nailed the list of 17 nonnegotiable demands to Dr. Peabody.

1972 – Jerome Duffin has been appointed Publisher and Owner of *Okra World*, a monthly journal charting the "ever-changing, dynamic industry of okra farming." Friends and classmates wishing to submit articles should write to Jerry directly. Only submissions dealing with okra, kale, or related produce will be considered. No poetry.

1975 – Roger Culver grows mushrooms and spiders in his cellar. He boils cats for the skeletons and bites the legs off live salamanders. Rog is a notorious ghoul, and frankly he is one alumnus we would just as soon did not keep us posted on his activities.

1978 – Robert Proctor was struck by lightning March 4 while fishing for bluegill on Moon Lake. When he was revived, he spoke only French and claimed to be the Vicomte de Chateaubriand, a French nobleman living in the 18th century. The Vicomte is back at work in his hardware store now and is studying English at night school. Bob's wife has adjusted to the transformation and is generally pleased. "Bob's manners have improved remarkably," she writes. "Our marriage has been revitalized and the kids are thrilled. Though I wish he hadn't started them in on that fencing."

1984 – Heroin addict Maynard Barshay has joined a methadone maintenance program in New Rochelle, New York. When he is able, Nard enjoys sailing on Long Island Sound.

1986 – George Whiter, reserve halfback for the 1985 league runner-ups, has been convicted of first-degree homicide in the shotgun slaying of his lovely wife Dottie (B.A., Bennington). George is awaiting execution in a Texas prison, and invites friends and classmates in the Lone Star state to drop by any time before June 13.

1987 – Bernard Stephenson underwent surgery April 7 and subsequently changed his name to Bernice Stephenson. The editors regret we shall be unable to print any further correspondence from Ms. Stephenson as the college, throughout its long and distinguished history, has been an institution open to males only. Friends and classmates interested in following the career of Ms. Stephenson are directed to the pages of the *National Enquirer*.

1991 – David Bruning applies pinstripes to rollerskaters in Venice, California. Last fall he spent several days decorating Elvira. Dave formerly was an assistant professor at California Institute of Technology. What made him change? It's hard to say. He may be high on something; so many of our younger alumni seem to be.

1995 – Arthur Barrett lives in a limestone cave near Squa Pan, Maine. He fashions his own clothes from wild hemp, grinds acorns for flour, brews beer from wild hops, hunts rabbits with a homemade bow and arrow, and is generally making a complete ass of himself up in the woods. Come on, Art. Grow up!

1996 – Darryl Chambers has officially retired, and is now dividing his time between his ranch in Montana and his home in Santa Fe. He was able to retire so young thanks to the worldwide popularity of his song "I'll Love You Always . . . In the Back Seat of My Car," recorded by Darryl and his garage band back in high school. "Call me a one-hit wonder," Darryl writes, "I could care less as long as those big royalty checks keep rolling in."

1999 – Recent grad Herbert Maxwell writes he is unable to find employment and has become mired in depression. "I'm beginning to wonder," notes young Herb, "if there really is any point to this struggle. What is it anyway we hope to attain in this polluted, crowded, tainted world? Why this mad scramble for success, for possessions, for status? What's the point?" Only point we can see, Herb, is the one poking out from under your hat. Listen, Herb, this old world doesn't owe you anything. If you want something, dammit, you're just going to have to wade in with your fists and fight for it. The sooner you learn that, young man, the sooner you'll have something really worthwhile to report to your alumni magazine. Well, how about it? We're waiting.

Rules of Play

The game is not difficult to learn if you are patient and read through the instructions step-by-step. So many of the people who write to us of their rage and frustration in failing to understand the game simply haven't taken the time to read the rules all the way through before commencing play. They blunder their way through the opening moves, happy as a lark, and then like as not roll a double-six while their blue marker is still in the secondary target zone, forfeiting their yellow marker *and* their vital green marker. A defense so decimated seldom survives beyond the third or fourth attack sortie unless the opposition is very naive indeed. Sharp players will pounce with alacrity (and merit no censure for their ruthlessness!) when so choice a target is laid out so pitifully defenseless before them. TO AVOID THE ANGUISH OF PRE-MATURE OBLITERATION, READ THE INSTRUCTIONS CAREFULLY BEFORE COMMENCING PLAY. We can say no more.

The game may be played by as few as two people, though it will quite tedious and hardly worth the trouble of setting up, or by as many as ten people, when the excitement can become un-bearable. Keep in mind the tensions of this game can seem quite real to some people. Be careful. If you have a narrow table, don't go cramming a lot of people around it and expect to play a nice demure game. Uncomfortable people can be snappish, and snappish people in contentious situations can become dangerous. Crowd a lot of your friends together in a hot room and they can turn on each other like mad dogs. We've seen it happen. TO KEEP IT COOL, KEEP IT COMFORTABLE.

Plush chairs are better than hard folding chairs. They are easier on the seat and much less likely to be picked up and heaved. Benches are terrible. With people lined up in rows the temptation to cheat becomes irresistible. Cheating leads to quarrels and QUARRELS LEAD TO VIOLENCE.

Play it safe. Establish at the beginning of the game that cheating will not be tolerated and DON'T BACK DOWN. Vacillation on this point always leads to strife. Someone inevitably rises to test your resolve. Remember: People who are behind in the game HAVE NOTHING TO LOSE. They will cheat if they think they can get away with it. EVEN FAMILY MEMBERS! If you let them and they beat you, IT'S YOUR OWN FAULT.

This is a game of strategy and skill, but luck is still a factor. If luck seems to turn against you, don't give way to despair. A sullen, dejected person will not be able to concentrate and will miss many choice opportunities to score. Remain optimistic, watch the markers carefully, accept any setbacks as temporary, and sooner or later your luck will change. When it does, you'll be in a position to dish it out like you had to take it. Remember: a stoic sufferer tastes a sweeter revenge.

When you are ahead in points, guard against complacency. A few victories, especially in the early skirmishes before the defenses are set, can lead to overconfidence. If you are smiling and cracking jokes, you cannot be watching the board. Smugness breeds inattentiveness which leads to calamity which ends in disaster. Get up on your high horse and YOU ARE RIDING FOR A FALL. You've been warned.

Accurate score-keeping is essential to the enjoyment of the

game. The scorekeepers must be mathematically inclined and have neat, legible handwriting. Note we said scorekeeper*s*. Both teams must have an equal voice in keeping score; thus joint score-keeping is essential. Let one side keep score exclusively and you are opening a Pandora's box THAT CAN ONLY END TRAGICALLY. One red marker disregarded or noted surreptitiously as a yellow marker can defeat hours of careful strategy. Don't be a victim: DEMAND AN EQUAL VOICE IN KEEPING SCORE. It's your right.

The game has been carefully designed to minimize procedural conflicts, but—nonetheless—disputes over permissibility of moves sometimes occur, even in championship play. These disputes should be resolved through nonviolent arbitration. Please do not telephone, fax, or e-mail us seeking rulings on procedural disputes. Appoint a representative from each team to arbitrate the matter along with a neutral third party. Neighbors are always happy to give of their time to settle disputes, if approached in a calm, polite, non-agitated manner. Do *not* call 911—the paramedics will not know what you are talking about and in the ensuing confusion may apply the "paddles of life" to your chest. It's happened before.

Give tempers a chance to cool before commencing arbitration. Try to find a private area where the arbiters can meet without fear of being overheard. This is essential if you are to avoid intimidation or corruption of the arbiters. A CORRUPT DECISION IS WORSE THAN NO DECISION AT ALL. Protect your arbiters. Guard against harassment. Let them decide the issues—that's what they're there for. Volunteer testimony only if it is sought by the arbitration panel and then try to conduct yourself in a dignified manner. Remember: you are an adult (unless you are, in fact, a child; see Appendix for special Children's Rules). Let reason prevail, not emotion. When the arbiters announce their decision, swallow your rage and accept their judgment. VENT YOUR

AGGRESSIONS ON THE PLAYING BOARD, NOT ON YOUR OPPONENTS.

You are now ready to play the game. Approach it carefully, with an open mind, and you'll find it an immensely rewarding and pleasurable experience. Approach it petulantly, with a chip on your shoulder, and you're in for a mean and dismal time. If you don't like the game, MAYBE IT'S NOT THE GAME.

Maybe it's you.

Watch the Birdie

9:00 a.m. I awake under the impression I am William Powell. Passing a mirror I am startled to discover someone shaved off my mustache during the night. Checking my body for tattoos, I discover my true identity. I am relieved. I pull back my "Sleep with the Stars" satin bed sheets. Sure enough a slight depression can be seen where my head had rested on the star marked "Myrna Loy."

9:05 a.m. I fish my morning newspaper out of a puddle on the front stoop. Placing the soggy mass in the microwave, I dart upstairs for a quick shower and shave. My upstairs neighbor, Mr. Bontone, asks why I do not use my own bathroom. I once again explain that any dampness in my apartment exacerbates the incipient wave in my hair.

9:30 a.m. I prepare my favorite breakfast—instant oatmeal, instant coffee, and Tang. It only takes an instant. Retrieving my now-dry newspaper, I discover the boy has left, not today's *Times* but yesterday's Des Moines *Register-Tribune*. Nevertheless I read through the "help wanted" classified section and note smugly there are no jobs in Iowa for which I am qualified.

10:45 a.m. Overcome by a powerful craving for a toasted danish, I stroll to the bakery, but never make it. Rude arms grasp my person and a handkerchief doused with Jade East cologne is held against my nose.

11:15 a.m. I regain consciousness in the back seat of a moving automobile. It is traveling across the Brooklyn Bridge. My heart is seized with fear. I have never been to Brooklyn before. "Uh, there must be some mistake," I stammer, addressing the two burly men in the front seat.

"Hey, don't yuz worry none, man," replies the driver, "Me and Mario's gonna take good care of yuz." Mario grunts in assent, giving me what I interpret as a wink in the rearview mirror. Like his partner he is big—six feet of muscle separate the black pumps from the greasy pompadour—with a face suggesting an unfortunate overexposure to gun butts and acid.

"Hey, who said you could take off yuz blindfold?" demands the driver.

"What blindfold?" I reply.

"Dammit, Phil! We forgot the blindfold," mutters Mario. "OK, dude, shut your eyes. And no peeking!"

Terrified, I close my eyes.

12:10 p.m. My eyes still squeezed firmly shut, I am hustled out of the car and up a steep flight of stairs reeking of unwashed banisters. I hear an iron door close behind me and sneak a peek. My kidnapers don't seem to mind.

"Well, man, make yuzself at home," says Mario, locking a steel girder across the door and placing the key in a leather pouch concealed in his hair. "It is me and Phil's desire to make yuz visit here as comfortable and pleasant as possible."

Phil beams in assent and adds affably, "Yuz wish is our command and vicy-versy I'm sure."

While pondering the import of that cryptic statement, I gaze wearily about the grim room where for reasons I know not I am to be held prisoner. An involuntary shudder wracks my body as my aesthetic sensibilities are pummeled mercilessly. Walter Keene children and cats in shades of pink and green peer out from the tattered wallpaper on the rear wall, dolefully contemplating their reflections in the gold-veined mirror tiles covering the front wall. Rows of imitation brick alternate with strips of lavender and tan aluminum siding on the right wall. Sheets of imitation marble surmounted by toga-clad plaster cupids cover the left wall, pierced by two grime-encrusted windows overlooking a paper box factory, booming with the industrial thuds of crimpers, folders, and giant guillotine blades. An iron bedframe painted to resemble mahogany and bearing a sagging mattress concealed under a fake tiger skin rises in the center of the room above a sea of electric orange shag carpet. Over the bed a blond Crosley television-phonograph console looms threateningly, suspended from the ceiling by skimpy bungee cords. Various outcroppings of painted metal tables and chairs round out the room's furnishings, along with a cigarette pockmarked padded-vinyl wet bar. A 500-watt sodium vapor lamp suspended by a black lace brassiere in the center of the sparkle-flecked ceiling blazes with an intensity rivaling high noon on the planet Venus.

2:30 p.m. As Mario and Phil have ignored my repeated entreaties for an explanation of why I am being held captive, I am resigned to making the best of the situation. We rearrange the furniture to create a conversation pit and Mario sets to work mending some holes in the tiger skin. While Phil disinfects the bathroom, I give the place a thorough dusting. The first floor of the building, I soon discover, is occupied by a bowling alley. From the periodic rumblings beneath the floor I deduce we are directly above Alley Four. When the household chores are completed, Phil is sent out for some lunch. He returns with a frozen tuna noodle casserole and bag of stale cake doughnuts.

"Sorry, der's no cookin' allowed in da rooms," Phil apologizes, handing me a doughnut and a chunk of casserole. Sucking moodily on my frigid lunch, I wander over to a shelf of books bound in distressed Naugahyde. Expecting the complete works of Macaulay or Ruskin, I find instead a 20-volume home-study course in insurance underwriting. While my captors match wits over a chess board (playing tic-tac-toe on the squares), I pass the next hour sullenly perusing a volume entitled *The Vagaries of Disability Claim Enforcement*.

4:00 p.m. Scoring 28 out of a possible 100 points on "Compensation of Victims of Wars, Plagues, and Natural Disasters: A Self-administered Test," I conclude I have no future in underwriting and reluctantly abandon my studies. I switch on the television set, which receives only a Hoboken station broadcasting Spanish language soap operas. The blurry, black and white picture rolls in rhythm with the buzzing red neon "Bowl" sign blinking on and off outside the window.

7:05 p.m. My head and eyes ache from the glare of the overhead light and I'm feeling a little queasy from watching the rolling picture on the television, but I am able to eat a little dinner and my spirits are holding up better than might be expected. Dinner consists of an anchovy and pineapple pizza Mario brought back from the lunchroom of a nearby bus station washed down with the rest of the doughnuts. I feel like taking a nap, but Mario and Phil seem anxious that I not fall asleep. Phil's setting up a card table now and we're all going to try to put together a 3,000-piece jigsaw puzzle of Salvatore Dali's painting of the Last Supper. Mario's mixing us a cocktail he calls a Tequila Sunstroke— a purplish potation made with tequila, Dr. Pepper, Snappy Tom, whipped tofu, and a few other mystery ingredients he says he has taken an oath never to reveal.

Phil turns out to be something of a music lover. He's been playing a tape of Joe Cocker singing "I Shot the Sheriff (But I Did Not Shoot the Deputy)" over and over again for the past hour. I'm beginning to wish it was a case of murder-suicide.

10:15 p.m. We have most of the banquet table pieced together and I'm working on my fifth Tequila Sunstroke. Phil and Mario are very congenial company and the evening has been fall of lively conversation and good cheer. They say if I have any more trouble with my stomach, one of then will go out and try to find a drugstore. Despite the time I've spent in the bathroom, I've fit three pieces for every two they've added and they both agree they're glad I'm here working on this thing with them. I explain I have always believed if you're going to do something, you might as well try to do the best job you can.

1:30 a.m. I am very, very tired and I've been bleeding a little from the ears and nose, but Phil and Mario are determined to finish the puzzle and I don't want to let them down. I doubt if I could sleep much anyway. This is league night for the shift that got off at midnight at the paper box factory and they've been racking up strikes and raising a ruckus downstairs for the past hour. I am told they sometimes bowl until dawn. Phil's playing his tape again to help drown out the noise. I begged him to play something else, but he just looked hurt and chewed on his cigar. Speaking of noxious vapors, Mario's been smoking a tobacco mixture called "Cherry Cheesecake" in his pipe for most of the evening and he insists I'll catch my death of cold if we open a window. I'm a little hoarse now from breathing through my mouth.

4:30 a.m. I'm still very tired but the red capsules are beginning to have some effect. Mario got them downstairs. I guess they're what's keeping all those bowlers going too. We've been making a lot of silly mistakes with the puzzle. We had a piece of grapefruit stuck on Luke's face for more than an hour before someone noticed it. I tell Mario and Phil if they're not going to pay attention, to get their own damn puzzle to work on. Both are sulking now.

6:40 a.m. The puzzle is more than four-fifths complete. Even in this unfinished state you can tell it is an impressive work of art. Mario and Phil have been telling me their life stories. I am sworn to secrecy. We all agree if the details were ever known and the witnesses allowed to live, they'd both get a minimum of a thousand years, possibly more if the judge decided to make an example of them.

9:30 a.m. We are left with three pieces and three holes in the puzzle, but try as we might we cannot fit them into place. My head throbbing, no longer able to focus my eyes, I feel something snap in my mind. With an anguished cry I hurl the card table across the room and, pulling the window drapes down on top of me, I slump to the floor sobbing uncontrollably. Mario and Phil are surprisingly understanding. They say nothing and quietly clean up the mess. Gradually I claw my way back to the edge of reality. When the spasms wracking my body have subsided to an intermittent hiccough, Phil says in a gentle voice, "OK, pal. It's all over. Yuz is free to go now." I stare uncomprehendingly at him.

"Yeah," adds Mario, "any place yuz wants to go, we'll take yuz der."

I begin to understand. I am not to be held for ransom or viciously slain. "You'll—you'll take me home?" I sputter.

Mario and Phil exchange glances.

"Sure, we'll take yuz home—if dat's where yuz wants to go," replies Mario. "Dat is, if maybe der isn't someplace else yuz is supposed to go."

I try to think, my mind is swimming. "Well, I—I did have an appointment with a photographer this morning. But, but I couldn't possibly. . ."

"No, no," insists Phil, "we don't want to be da cause of yuz missin' out on any of yuz 'pointments. We'll take yuz to dis photographer fella."

My protests are useless. I am carried downstairs and bundled into the car for the drive back to Manhattan.

11:05 a.m. I am standing under a battery of glaring lights in front of a stark white background. My body trembles and a cold sweat trickles down my forehead. Over the roaring in my ears I can hear people walking about in the semidarkness beyond the lights. An arm reaches out of the gloom and holds a brownie near my mouth. Although the thought of food nauseates me, I decide to be polite and I bite down on a light meter. I feel someone wipe the spittle from my chin and hear him say, "Philippe, Maurice, I think we'll need another backfill spot on the right there." Two men walk near and adjust the lights. Their faces look familiar. Somewhere I have seen them. Long ago. I hear a camera shutter open and close. Someone says, "OK." My knees begin to buckle. The floor rushes up and bounces against me; I collapse into unconsciousness.

Epilogue: The prints arrived in the mail two days later. Although I had to concede that Mr. Avedon captured in many ways the essential nobility of my soul, I felt that on the whole the poses were distinctly unflattering. Fortunately, however, I had acquired over the years a certain facility with the airbrush, and through a few hours spent in pleasant labor I was able to improve the portraits tremendously.

Paragraphs for Sale

"Is this the room in which sits the gentleman who writes the paragraphs?"

"Yes. May I help you?"

"I hope so. I'd like to buy a paragraph."

"Of course. Have a seat."

"Thank you."

"We're having a special this month on chapters: two for $39.95."

"No, thanks. I think a paragraph should be sufficient."

"Very well. What is it you wish to record?"

"My life story."

"Hmmm. Yes, I think a paragraph should do nicely. Shall we begin then? When were you born?"

"I was born in a time of innocence: a simpler age, now nearly forgotten, when the world was new and life glowed with the golden luster of hope."

"I see. When precisely was that?"

"Uh, 1939."

"Fine. And where were you born?"

"I was born in a magical city on the shores of a great blue lake—a city where a million happy souls laughed and loved, struggled and frolicked, sang their songs, and dreamt their dreams."

"That was . . ."

"Cleveland, Ohio."

"Right, Cleveland. And your parents were?"

"My father was a great man, a strong man—hearty in voice and spirit with a gentle laugh and a deep reverence for antiquity."

"He was . . ."

"A mortician."

"Fine. And your mother?"

"My mother was a vision in white: a tiny woman, delicate of limb, but fierce of will, with a golden smile that lit up the room and filled my youthful heart with sunshine."

"She was a housewife?"

"Uh, yes."

"You went to school?"

"Yes. There my innocent eyes were first opened to the wonders of the greater world. As if by magic, one-by-one the doors of literature, mathematics, and science were flung open and their rich treasures heaped at my feet."

"You majored in?"

"Welding."

"I see. And when you graduated?"

"Suddenly, I had my manhood thrust upon me. It was time to renounce the simple joys of childhood and accept the responsibilities of citizenship."

"You were drafted?"

"Yes. By the United States Army: the most awesome fighting force the world has ever known—an elite corps of citizen warriors forged into one invincible sword by the iron hammer of discipline, each day facing death calmly, without remorse, to safeguard the freedoms of a great people."

"You were a . . ."

"Latrine attendant, second class."

"And when you were discharged?"

"I returned to the city of my birth, a boy no longer, but now a man—with a man's body and a man's passions."

"You had to get married?"

"Yes, but I loved Edna. Sort of."

"Your wife is . . ."

"A vigorous woman, stout of heart and limb, independent of mind, confident in her opinions, never shirking from the free expression of her thoughts."

"She's a fat nag?"

"Some might put it that way, yes."

"And your child?"

"Oh, a saucy youth, bold and forthright, with a wholesome disdain for the pretensions and strictures of a society grown fat and listless in its senility."

"He's a young hoodlum?"

"So his parole officer asserts."

"Have you any other children?'"

"Alas, that is our great sorrow: that in the garden of our blessed union only a single flower has bloomed."

"Your wife refuses to sleep with you?"

"Yes, but only for the past twelve years."

"And your job is—what?"

"Like all men born into this world, I seek my place, my niche, where I may take up the tools God has given me, roll back my sleeves, and commit my energies, my talents, and my dreams to productive labor."

"You're unemployed?"

"Yes. Things are a bit slow in the welding business at the moment."

"You last worked—when?"

"Uh, 1973."

"Yes, well, I think we have quite an adequate paragraph here. Would you care to examine it?"

"Yes, if I may. Oh, it's quite well done. I wish I had your way with words."

"It's an innate talent honed by years of experience and training. Now don't forget we offer a ten-day home trial period. If in that period you should decide that the paragraph is unsatisfactory, you may return it and exchange it for another paragraph of equal or lesser value."

"Oh, I'm sure this one will do quite well, thank you."

"Yes, it certainly should. And if, through some extraordinary circumstance, you experience another noteworthy incident in your life, please don't hesitate to come back. We'll write you a second paragraph—for half price."

"That shall be my ambition then, my hope, my dream: a sunny mountain peak looming enticingly on a distant horizon to lure me forward along the rocky paths of life."

"A goal."

"Yes, that's it. Well, good day."

"Good day to you, sir. It's been a pleasure."

Too Young Too Late

Have you been catching up with those old movies on cable? You soon discover that in Hollywood "old" is a relevant term.

For example, the other night you may have seen *Faithless* (1932), a Depression-era comedy in which Tallulah Bankhead and Robert Montgomery play impoverished society swells struggling to scrape up carfare. At one point Tallulah is asked her age. "Twenty-four," she admitted with modest sincerity.

Yeah, right.

Miss Bankhead may have been 24 at some point in her life, but I suspect it was long before talking pictures arrived on the scene.

That same week brought us *The Ambassador's Daughter* (1956), starring Olivia De Havilland as a dewy-eyed Parisian maiden resisting the advances of dashing enlisted man John Forsythe. This was 17 years after Olivia swiped Ashley Wilkes from Scarlett in *Gone with the Wind* and 21 years after her movie debut in *The Irish in Us* (1935). Two decades later, Miss De Havilland looked fetching in her Dior wardrobe, but you may have noticed the director never moved in very close on his ingenue. Perhaps it was because she was celebrating her fortieth birthday that year.

Also young behind its years is *Inside Daisy Clover* (1965), the story of a troubled tomboy aspiring to teen stardom in 1930s Hollywood. At least adolescent Daisy didn't have to worry about pimples. That 15-year-old starlet was played by 27-year-old Natalie Wood.

Hollywood leading men engage in age-fudging too. Take the case of *Susan Slept Here* (1954), in which playboy screenwriter Dick Powell suddenly finds himself married to juvenile delinquent Debbie Reynolds. Should he keep her? The problem is that the child bride is only 17, while the groom is "19 years older." According to my pocket calculator, that would make Dick a still-youthful 36.

Yeah, right.

In fact, Dick Powell had 28 years seniority on Debbie. In 1954 she was a bubbling 22 and he was mature 50. Can this marriage be saved? I doubt it.

A half-century later, actors are still playing fast and loose with their ages. For example, if her official biography is to be believed, former "Cheers" star Kirstie Alley is now four years younger than everyone else in her high-school class. "That's odd," former classmates have commented, "she didn't look 14 when we graduated."

The good news is that there's no reason why the rest of us can't readjust our ages to Hollywood time. According to my official biography, I am now a vigorous 34. And no, I will not be attending any high-school reunions with my aging peers.

Are You Camping?

"Camping out" is the term my wife uses for folks like us whose living arrangements lack those essential finishing touches. Alas, she has been camping out her entire married life. Though we have been in our present house nearly five years, the living room still sports gold-veined mirror tiles and fake wood paneling, the kitchen is a festival of disco-era browns, and assorted wallpapers from hell accent other rooms. My wife is eager to remodel, but I think it would be less stressful just to post a large sign proclaiming: "The decor of this house does not necessarily reflect the taste of its occupants."

Here is a short test to determine if you too are camping out:

Your computer sits on a card table, +5 points. It sits on the box it came in, +10 points.

Your books are stacked on bricks and boards, +5 points. Your books are strewn across the premises, +10 points.

The last time you were in a thrift shop you were: Dropping off designer discards, -5 points. Ducking in out of the rain, 0 points. Shopping for bargains, +5 points. Greeted by name by the sales clerk, +10 points.

Your home is more "animal barn" than Pottery Barn, +5 points.

A blanket covers your hand-me-down couch, +5 points. The blanket features NFL team logos, +10 points.

Embroidered hand towels hang in your guest bathroom, -5 points.

The dominant aroma in your home is: Eau de kennel, +5 points. Rose potpourri, -5 points. Methamphetamine brewing, +15 points.

You subscribe to *Architectural Digest*, -5 points.

Posters are thumbtacked to your walls, +5 points. The posters are of Metallica, +10 points.

Your mattress is: On a solid wood bed, -5 points. On the floor: +5 points. On the back porch: +10 points.

In your two-car garage you have space to park: Two cars, -5 points. One car, 0 points. Not even a bicycle, +10 points.

Your bathroom can best be described as: Color-coordinated, -5 points. Eclectic, 0 points. Grungy, +5 points. A pit, +10 points.

You own a book on *feng shui*, -5 points. You've actually read it, -10 points.

Your neighbors have: Asked you for decorating advice, -10 points. Offered to loan you a lawn mower, +5 points. Reported you to zoning authorities, +10 points. Threatened to fire-bomb your house, +20 points.

Teenagers are in the home, +30 points.

Your house is equipped with wheels, +40 points.

RATE YOUR SCORE:

0 to 25 points: Martha Stewart would be proud.

25 to 50 points: Caution, some camping detected.

50+ points: Greetings, fellow campers!

Ask Mr. Rentsit

Q – Can I rent my socks?

A – Yes. Many people are earning a nice second income renting out their hosiery. As I pointed out in my book, *Rent Your Assets*, the average person has several thousand dollars invested in wearing apparel—an investment that can be made to yield big dividends. All clothing can be rented out; the supply has not yet begun to catch up with demand. People who run short of socks will pay good money to rent a nice pair of argyles. Even those wretched ties your relatives gave you can be rented successfully. You'd be surprised how many people there are with appalling taste who'd love to rent your horrible ties for a day or so. Seasonal garments should never be left lying idle in closets or trunks. When the warm weather returns, I lease my overcoat and galoshes to a thrift-minded estate agent in New Zealand. The extra wear is minimal, and sometimes when the garments are returned I find a nice surprise or two in the pockets.

Q – I was quite popular with the young ladies in my day and accumulated several hundred torrid love letters. Is there any way I can make money from these?

A – Certainly. There are thousands of lonely men around the country who would love to receive spicy mash notes on a rental basis. A few dollars for photocopying and some inexpensive toilet water and you're in business. Go to it!

Q – I tried to rent your book, *Rent This Book*, and was tossed out of the bookshop on my ear. What's the story?

A – You apparently failed to read far enough. The complete title of my new book is *Rent This Book . . . To Your Friends for Fun and Profit*. It tells you how to put your home library to work for you instead of sitting there gathering dust. Also included are chapters with valuable hints on renting out your high school yearbook, old scrapbooks, back issues of agricultural and girlie magazines, and yesterday's newspaper.

Q – Having suffered some dire reverses in the market I am left with nothing but my good name. What should I do?

A – Shady characters, whose own names are loathed by all decent persons, will pay top dollar for the use of a good name. Be prepared, though, to be snubbed by your friends.

Q – My husband gave me this expensive food processor for Christmas, but now he says if he sees one more bowl of coleslaw around here he's going to decorate the kitchen walls with it. Don't tell me to make carrot-raisin salad instead because Randy says he got enough of that "miserable glop" in the Navy. I'd hate just to park this machine because it was expensive and I read in a magazine that grinding vegetables relieves stress. Can I rent it out?

A – You bet. I get hundreds of letters every month from coleslaw fanatics wanting to know where they can rent food processors. But why let someone else have all the fun? Your machine can make money for you right there in your kitchen. I know of a woman in Dayton who made eight thousand dollars last year grinding vegetables to order for her neighbors and got off Prozac to boot.

Q – I was drunk last night and a smooth-talking sharpie talked me into buying a dead elephant carcass. Is this rentable?

A – Carnival owners tell me there is a slow but steady demand in their profession for elephant carcasses as crowd teasers. Of course, you probably would have been wiser to have leased the carcass as its income-earning potential is likely to decline sharply as time goes by. I suggest you donate it soon to your local food bank and be content with the whopping tax deduction.

Q – Through a contact I can't divulge I have the opportunity to lay my hands on a rare kinescope of the complete gavel-to-gavel coverage by the Dumont Network of the 1952 Republican National Convention. I hear there's going to be a big Eisenhower boom soon. Should I try to cash in?

A – By all means. My sources in trend centers tell me we are just a few months away from a great revival of interest in the late general. The cultural impact will be profound, with a sudden revival of baggy trousers, those strange jackets, and men buttoning the top button of their plaid sport shirts. Smart operatives already have moved into the thrift shops and are snapping up every Ike badge and button they can find. Prices are skyrocketing. A kinescope of the general at his moment of greatest political triumph should have fantastic rental potential. And don't overlook the long-term Dick Nixon dividends.

Q – I have a large autographed photograph of Tom Jones (the singer, not the other one). Is this rentable?

A – Autographed Tom Jones photographs, although far from rare, can be rented successfully. Many people, though they might not care to own one outright, would enjoy having such a memento in their home for a few days.

Q – My wife's brother is the most obnoxious person in the world. Somebody told me there are agencies which rent out obnoxious people as novelties for parties. Where do I go to sign this guy up?

A – Several agencies like this were started, but I believe all of them have folded. Party-givers discovered that once the drinking began in earnest they generally had a sufficient number of obnoxious persons among the invited guests.

Q – Although I am but eight years old, I am remarkably intelligent for my age as I trust you are able to discern from this missive which I have penned without the assistance of my parental forebears. I enjoy your books and column very much and for several years have been successfully renting out my homework. I'd like to expand and was wondering what you think of the opportunities for a smart child in the rental export market to Japan?

A – The opportunities are good, but you must act quickly. Several children have entered this field already and are racking up impressive grosses renting baseball trinkets and comic books to the youth overseas.

Q – I don't have a question, but I do have a rental success story to share with you and your readers. When I moved into my new apartment, I decided my wet bar was a valuable asset that could be put to work yielding dividends. So I went to the supermarket and bought a dozen bottles of liquor and then invited all my friends over for a housewarming party. Well, they were a little surprised when they found out I was charging for drinks, but after a few moments of embarrassed silence they decided it was a great idea after all because my prices were cheaper than most bars and I gave out free popcorn. Now my "bar" is open every weekend and I have more friends—and money—than I know what to do with. The rental life is grand—and I owe it all to you.

A – Thank you for your heartwarming testimonial. Yes, the rental life is grand and "renting" your wet bar is a great idea. But are you sure you want to give away snacks? An attractive buffet, reasonably priced, might be far more popular with your friends— and beneficial to your cashbox—than free munchies. And on those occasions when friends over imbibe and can't be trusted to find their way home, don't overlook those other assets you can rent— like that sofa, those pajamas, and that toothbrush.

Q – Every time I rent out my home psychoanalysis tapes, Album Seventeen ("Groping for Guilt") comes back broken. Is there some way I can prevent cathartic violence from eating into my rental income?

A – According to Dr. Lyle Freebling, who developed the home psychanalysis series and flogs it on late night television, Album Seventeen has proven to be something of a "hot potato" in the "directed aggression" department and has been recalled. A new Album Seventeen, "Harmonize Your Hang-ups," has been issued and may be ordered from Dr. Freebling at his post office box in Reno.

Q – My husband passed on this year, leaving me with no insurance, the meagerest of pensions, and two thousand four hundred and nineteen wooden ironing boards collected with single-minded zeal over the previous six decades. Owning a nice (metal) ironing board myself and being somewhat strapped for funds I tried auctioning them off, but received no bids. Can I rent them out?

A – Otis Flybacker, president of the Wooden Ironing Board Collectors of America (WIBCA), says your late husband's collection, although not large by professional standards, contains many interesting examples, including a very rare 1908 oak and nickel, wall-hung Auto-Fold-Junior—a board he claims is "practically priceless." The present depressed market for ironing apparatus he attributes to "temporary collector fatigue" induced by recent frantic price escalations and the proliferation of counterfeits on Ebay. Mr. Flybacker strongly recommends against renting out your boards, as he has seen some "tragic cases" of rare boards ruined through careless ironing. Instead, he suggests you have the boards professionally crated and store them in a fireproof, humidity-controlled warehouse for a few years until the market revives. Though it is always painful to see rentable assets lie fallow, perhaps in this one instance that would be the wisest course. We mustn't be dogmatic about these things.

Lyle's Party

I should never have gone to that party. I hate parties. But you can't just hole up in your room all the time. That last sentence I hear in my mother's voice, loaded like a freight train with emotional baggage. The party was way down the peninsula, practically to San Jose. I wouldn't have gone, but my friend Adriane can play my insecurities like a harp.

"There will be lots of single men there, Wendy," she promised. "Attractive single men with hefty stock options and . . ." *Bad static.*

"I didn't get that last lie, Adriane," I replied. "Your cellular connection is breaking up."

"Affluent lifestyles," she repeated.

"Lots of nerds, you mean. Greasy workaholic geeks on the prowl for babes half our age."

"Not geeks, Wendy," she insisted. "These guys are in the financial end. Most of them went to b-school like Tod."

Adriane's one-eyed boyfriend Tod drove us down in his new Saab. I mention his infirmity not to flout the American with Disabilities Act, but to explain why riding with Tod makes me nervous. He has deep-set eyes and a big Latin nose, which means that everything to the left of the steering wheel is a complete mystery to the guy. So he compensates by getting in the fast lane and flooring it. Even in heavy traffic he tailgates and flashes his lights at the drivers ahead as if his MBA granted him a dispensation from highway congestion. It's classic asshole behavior in my book, but Adriane says if you want a successful, aggressive male, you have to accept the testosterone overflow.

Tod's wireless Palmtop was reporting delays on the Bay Bridge (no surprise there), so he zoomed south on the Nimitz and crossed over the San Mateo Bridge. The house we were looking for was on a woodsy street in an exclusive neighborhood uphill from Menlo Park. The party was in full swing and the narrow, winding lane was jammed with pricey cars, all foreign models except for the usual SUVs. Tod made one quick circuit of the block then backed his Saab up against the front bumper of a pearlescent white Lexus, setting off its alarm.

"Get back! Get back!" shrieked an anguished synthesized voice. Tod drove forward an inch. The shrieking stopped. We were partially blocking the driveway of the neighboring house (and completely immobilizing the Lexus), but Tod left this hastily scribbled note under his windshield wiper: "Party! Come find me. Sorry — Tod."

It was one of those parties where no one gets introduced, but the music wasn't loud enough or fast enough to dance to. You're expected to hang around and converse with total strangers, most of whom are married or otherwise entangled, which doesn't stop them from checking you out the minute you step inside the door. The first thing I did after grabbing a glass of warm chardonnay was join the line outside the one bathroom. My tipsy line-mate explained that the house was purchased as a tear-down, but Lyle's IPO got delayed by a sudden market dip. Lyle was the pony-tailed birthday boy turning 50 that day. His house was a compact stucco ranch about the same vintage as its owner. Someone had dressed up the sheetrock with a ragged finish, which always makes me nervous for some reason. It may be a tear-down, but compared to my tiny Berkeley apartment it was a palace. At the very least, I thought, cheapskate Lyle could have chilled his wine, hired a real band, and rented a porta-potty or two.

When I finally returned from the bathroom, Adriane was circulating through the rooms and discreetly adjusting the lighting to more flattering levels. I switched to red wine and floated about the living room hoping my eyes were shining bright, my diamond earrings were sparkling, and my revealing neckline wasn't too blatant for Silicon Valley. I hovered alluringly here and there, but the earnestly conversing guests seldom glanced my way. They were as evenly paired off as penguins on an Antarctica beach.

Do people really meet future life-partners at parties? It theoretically must be possible, though I've yet to encounter anyone who has. Adriane met Tod at a seminar on investment strategy—not that they're married and not that Adriane has any money to invest. I met Fred when he stormed out of the kitchen in his cute apron to inquire why I'd sent back the seared tuna. I said, "Do I look Japanese? I don't eat raw fish." Of course, living in Berkeley I eat sushi all the time, but context is everything. You don't expect to follow your caesar salad in that kind of restaurant with a bloody slab of under-cooked fish.

Fred's the only guy (so far) who's asked me to marry him. After nearly three years together, he announced one morning that he was returning to his hometown of Harrisburg, Pennsylvania to open a restaurant with a college buddy, and said if I wanted to move with him, we'd better get married because his parents were very old-fashioned. Not a proposal steeped in romance, but I tormented myself for two whole weeks before declining. I liked Fred, I loved his mastery in the kitchen, but I couldn't see myself relocating to a place that deliberately chose to refer to itself as a "burg." A year or so later, I got a postcard from Kona. Fred and his friend had changed their plans and opened their restaurant in Hawaii. I don't make a cult of bitterness, but let me note that Fred's introduction to the islands came on a trip *I* paid for to celebrate our first anniversary together. The bastard's never even invited me to visit.

By 11:30 I had sipped three more glasses of wine, peed twice in the scrubby garden, and kissed a married Korean engineer with cigarette breath and busy hands. He cornered me on the deck while his chubby American wife was marooned in the bathroom line. Fifteen minutes before he had been telling me about his precocious nine-year-old daughter and her savvy investments—an odd buildup to seduction if you ask me. I kissed him back to be polite, but then that's probably one of my problems. I retreated to the kitchen and hung out with my new pals Jennie and Phil, who decided that very night to become engaged. We drank to their happiness. They're planning to fly to Las Vegas on Monday to get married, right after Jennie cancels her restraining order against him. Phil wasn't stalking her, she decided, he was just demonstrating his regard. He looked pretty harmless to me, but then it's those quiet, mild-mannered types who often turn out to be the real creeps.

With businesslike efficiency at 11:59 p.m. our host Lyle shot himself. I poured myself another drink and remained in the kitchen to escape all the uproar. Tod accompanied his bleeding friend to the hospital in the ambulance. When the cops arrived, I grabbed my purse and slipped out the back door with Adriane. She looked sober enough to drive, but Tod's car was not where we had left it.

"Someone stole poor Toddy's Saab!" she exclaimed.

"More likely it was towed," I replied. "Damn!"

Although it was a chilly spring night and neither of us had so much as a sweater, I followed Adriane down the hill. There were no sidewalks or streetlights. Large dogs barked menacingly from walled-in yards. Millionaires slept peacefully in pretentiously made-over houses, their security systems twinkling like electronic rubies beside the darkened front doors.

"Where are we going, Adriane?" I called.

No reply. My friend was not bending over that picket fence to pick roses, I realized. She was not as sober as I had thought. I dug through my purse and handed her a tissue.

"Sorry, Wendy," she gasped. "If we keep walking downhill, eventually we'll come to El Camino Real. The geography of the peninsula is extremely predictable."

"I don't know, Adriane. I'm cold and you neglected to tell me to wear my hiking boots to this party."

Adriane lurched off down the hill; I sighed and followed her.

"Well, I didn't know Lyle was going to shoot himself," she replied.

"Why did he do it, anyway?"

"Hey, the guy was 50, he was losing his hair, his girlfriend had just split, and all his venture capitalists had passed on phase two funding."

"Why didn't you tell me he was single, Adriane?"

"Wendy, you hate ponytails on men."

"Sure, doesn't everyone? But I could have overlooked it. The guy was semi-cute."

"Well, he's not very cute any more. He shot himself in the eye."

"No wonder Tod was so upset."

Adriane stopped. "Wendy, I can't believe you said that. Tod is very sensitive about his eye. He lost it playing racquetball."

"Adriane, in case you hadn't noticed, Tod is not here. We're alone on a freezing night, miles from nowhere. I say we knock on the closest door and call a cab."

"This is the 21st century, Wendy. If you knock on someone's door in the middle of the night, they'll immediately call 911, assuming they don't shoot you with their gun."

"So what if they call the cops," I pointed out. "The nice officers will give us a ride to a taxi stand."

"You mean they'll arrest us for prostitution. Have you looked in a mirror tonight, Wendy?"

"I'm not dressed like a hooker, Adriane. This is fashionable party wear."

"It's the same thing, girl," she sneered. "Get real."

Adriane was right about one thing. Eventually we did come to El Camino Real. Then we trudged on nearly to San Mateo as lonely men in expensive cars slowed to check us out. No one stopped. "We look like police decoys," reasoned Adriane, ever the optimist.

At last we came to an open Denny's. We had five cups of coffee to warm up, an overindulgence I regretted on the long, expensive cab ride back to the East Bay. I got sick and missed two weeks of work. Things turned out OK for Lyle though. He lost his eye, but got his phase two funding. Naturally, he and Tod are now best buddies. Lyle cut Tod in on his IPO, and they both became millionaires overnight. Too bad for Adriane that Tod dumped her. Last I heard she was running around with some divorced Korean engineer who made a big pile off his daughter's stock picks.

Death of a Poet

Cotton rope? No. Hemp. Must be hemp. Timeless material. The rough fibers twisted by skilled brown hands. How much? Six feet would do. Doubtless they make you buy at least fifty. A society built upon waste. Damn. No time for compromise. Be insistent. Two yards, no more. Still, might arouse suspicions. Suppose they have a way of knowing. Must deal with lots of people, nervous people desiring short lengths of rope. They can't take any chances. Liability problems. Relatives could sue. Suppose they call the police. Press notices would be grim: "The poet Rantone was arrested yesterday at Jim's Bait and Tackle Shop where he attempted to purchase a short length of hemp rope. It is believed he intended to employ the rope in taking his life. . ."

Damn. A belt? Yes, belt would do. Still, leather. Bad connotations. Sadism. Sex crimes. All those years of celibacy besmirched. Damn. Fabric? Fabric belt. Yes. Bedroom closet. Top shelf. Damn. Letters. Burn them? Just the carbons. Hide the originals. They'll find them eventually. Assume they were misplaced. A wonderful legacy miraculously preserved. Fabric belt. Fabric belt. Here. Damn. Sweat stains. Badminton must not be played in one's street clothes. Dry clean? Not enough time. God, the buckle. "The poet Rantone hanged himself yesterday. The corpse was discovered depending from a perspiration-stained fabric belt, the buckle of which bore the insignia of the Boy Scouts of America."

Damn. Ties? A possibility. Symbol of Capitalism. Conformity.

Materialism. God, these ties though. Mother has such rotten taste. Where does she find them? A plain blood-red tie. That would be good. Carmine. Moderate width. Silk. Yes, silk. Silk. Knotted silk scarves! Perfect. A touch of the East. Zen. Wonderful. Damn. Strong enough? Tensile strength of silk? Call the library, they'd know. Arouse curiosity, though. Damn. Should have been a goddam engineer. Silk, silk. Parachutes once made of silk. Must be strong. Good. Damn. Knots. Never could tie a decent knot. Find someone to tie them? Retired sailor maybe. Must be bars somewhere full of them. Engage one in conversation. Buy him a drink maybe. Good. Talk turns inevitably to knots. Pull out a couple of silk scarves. Mind showing me a few of your more intricate knots, my friend? Yeah, right. No way. Damn.

Knots. Knots, knots. Knots and knives. Mishima. Seppuku. Beheadings. Fountain of blood. Red pools in the snow. Ritual death. Damn. Pretentious for an Occidental. Derivative too. Damn. Knots, knives. The knell of death. Menacing—the marriage of those letters: K, N. The *keen* edge of the knife. The *k* and *n* separated by *ee*. Ee—the death cry. The Doppler effect. The pitch is observed to change as the body plummets through the void. A finite cry, but divisible into a billion parts. More than that. A billion billion intervals of time before the ghastly impact—the terminus of time and life against the concrete.

Damn. What if you live? Mutilated, but sentient. One could not help but be changed by the experience. "The poet Rantone has survived a plunge from the forty-seventh floor of the Prudential Building. Although horribly mutilated and crippled, he says he is happy to be alive and intends to devote the remainder of his life to easing the suffering of humankind around the world."

God. Rather be dead. Damn. Poison? Possible. The vessel of life is not sundered. No brooding presence of a closed casket to disturb the mourners. The face—so serene in death—a comfort to all. Cyanide? Good. How to obtain? Mail order? Perhaps the

JC Penney catalogue. Damn. Take too long. Questions for sure. Snotty order-takers in remote cubicles probing for evil intent. Damn. Drain cleaner? Kitchen. Cupboard under sink. Good. Almost full. *Caution: contains lye.* Lye! The desperate gulps searing the throat. The esophagus dissolving. The chest filling with blood pumped by the racing heart. Finally, the convulsions. The warm stomach debauched upon the chill linoleum. Lye: Death to life. Lie: Death to truth. A false death? Damn.

Stove? Gas. The inhalation of mephitic vapors. Sylvia Plath, dead in the grim London flat. An end to aspirations. Good. Yes, out with the rack. Here. A chair for the feet. No more awkward than sexual intercourse. Faint aromas assail the nose. The ghosts of potroasts past. Damn. The pilot's lit. Blow it out? There. Good. Not a bad fit. Push in a bit farther. Good. Damn. Where's the knob? *Kn!* There. Pretty comfortable, all things considered. Don't mind the smell of gas. Like garlic breath exhaled by an elephant. The top of the oven. Speckled. An infinity of tiny stars. I shall name the constellations. You. You are the stag with your antlers. You are the crab. You . . . Damn. Forgot to burn the letters. Damn. Too pleasant to move. Damn. Have to though. Damn. Oh, I'm floating. Kids by the millions should be sniffing this stuff. Letters. Letters. Where are you letters? Don't try to hide. There. Got you. Damn. Matches. I need matches. I need lots and lots of matches. No lighter either. Damn. Never should have pawned my gold Dunhill. Or quit smoking for that matter. Where are those damn matches? Oh, here's one.

C.D. Payne was born in 1949 in Akron, Ohio, the former "Rubber Capital of the World" famed for its tire factories. He shares a birthday with P.T. Barnum, a fact which has influenced his life profoundly. After graduating from Harvard College in 1971, he moved to California, where he's worked as a newspaper editor, graphic artist, cartoonist, typesetter, photographer, proofreader, carpenter, trailer park handyman, and advertising copywriter. He is married and lives in Sonoma County, north of San Francisco.

Acclaimed comic novels by C.D. Payne for your enjoyment

Frisco Pigeon Mambo

Discover these hard-drinking laboratory refugees, who as the infamous "Killer Pigeons" create havoc in San Francisco. They dance into bars, stick up liquor stores, dodge murder raps, and pull a miracle out of their hats. Will they find their way back home to Berkeley? Will they survive the next 15 minutes without a cigarette? Call them "America's Most Wanted," but don't call them pigeons. These swashbuckling outlaws think they're human. Soon to be a Twentieth-Century Fox animated feature film ("Party Animals") produced by the Farrelly brothers.

"The . . . seamless blend of high comedy and Wonder-landesque fantasy is uproarious." — *San Francisco* magazine.

($12.95 U.S., paper, ISBN: 1-882647-24-6.)

Civic Beauties

It's definitely not politics as usual as twin teenage sisters plot to "light a small cherry bomb" under their minister father's campaign for the Vice Presidency of the United States. While one lovely sister dallies with a picketing environmentalist, her identical twin conspires to "blow the elections sky high." The pace is hectic in this rollicking 'musical' novel as one surprising character after another suddenly breaks into "song."

"A witty, inventive, unique, engaging, laugh-a-minute novel of pure delight." — *Midwest Book Review.*

($12.95 U.S., paper, ISBN: 1-882647-20-3.)

Youth in Revolt: The Journals of Nick Twisp

Meet Nick Twisp, California's most precocious diarist, whose on-going struggles to make sense out of high school, deal with his divorced parents, and lose his virginity result in his transformation from an unassuming fourteen-year-old to a modern youth in open revolt. As his family splinters, worlds collide, and the police block all routes out of town, Nick must cope with economic deprivation, homelessness, the gulag of the public schools, a competitive Type-A father, murderous canines (in triplicate), and an inconvenient hair trigger on his erectile response. All the while, he must vie for the affections of the beauteous Sheeni Saunders, teenage goddess and ultimate intellectual goad.

"An unstintingly hilarious black comedy . . . has all the hallmarks of a classic." — *Los Angeles Times*.

($15.95 U.S., paper, ISBN: 0-385-48296-9.)

Revolting Youth: The Further Journals of Nick Twisp

Nick Twisp is back for more riotous adventures through the land mines of 21st century adolescence. This sequel finds love-struck Nick Twisp still on the lam from the law and his parents. Our teen hero (and his multiplying alter egos) now must battle blizzards, back-stabbing aliens, vengeful parents, and school officials determined to schedule him into girls' gym. He conspires to play cupid, journeys south of the border on a secret mission, takes gunplay lessons from his distraught mom, and still finds time to confide all to his diary while inadvertently wreaking havoc in cyberspace.

"This hilarious sequel will delight readers with its cast of eccentric teenagers, as will Nick's avaricious appetite for adjectives." — *Booklist*.

($14.95 U.S., paper, ISBN: 1-882647-15-7.)

Queen of America: A Royal Comedy

Welcome to the Kingdom of America, where a crisis in succession imperils the 220-year reign of the Washington royal family. Into the breach steps a lovely descendant of King George Washington I. She may become America's first Queen—if she can overcome the forces conspiring against her and prevent a war with her realm's fiercest adversary: the Kingdom of Canada.

Discover contemporary royal America, where athletes play polo on pogo sticks, tourists queue up to tour opulent palaces, shoppers spend millions on royal collectibles, and even Elvis earned a knighthood. In this fanciful and uproarious rewriting of history, the Czar of Russia is America's closest ally and behind every tree lurks a Canadian spy. Read C.D. Payne's first play—and get ready for a royal good time.

($9.95 U.S., paper, ISBN: 1-882647-10-6.)